I0544676

Manitoba Tea & Tarot Mysteries

MOVIES, MOONLIGHT & MAGIC

JANUARY BAIN

Movies, Moonlight & Magic
ISBN # 978-1-913186-21-0
©Copyright January Bain 2019
Cover Art by Erin Dameron-Hill ©Copyright September 2019
Interior text design by Claire Siemaszkiewicz
Totally Bound Publishing

MOVIES, MOONLIGHT & MAGIC

Dedication

It takes a huge team of support players to write a book. A brilliant editor, a fabulous publishing house, helpful friends and family, but most of all it comes down to the reader. This book is dedicated to all my fellow cozy lovers out there.

And as always, thank you to my darling husband, Don, for your undying love and belief. Right back at you, handsome!

Chapter One

"I've got it, Charm!" Star flew into the Tea & Tarot café, the ever-present star-pendant swinging wildly about her neck and a piece of paper clutched in her hand. The angel chimes holding court over the doorway accompanied her arrival, singing with enough enthusiasm to awaken the dead. Before I could move, she pulled me into a crushing hug, doing a spectacular impression of one of the black bears that our part of the world is renowned for.

"Slow down, sis. What's going on?" I pulled away to pick up the faded tea towel I'd dropped in the brouhaha.

"I got the part! You know, the movie? *Witches and Wolves*! Get with the program, sis. See? I got confirmation right here." She waved the crumpled piece of paper about as if it was a stock certificate. Maybe it was, for her. I had absolutely no interest in being in a movie, now or ever.

"What kind of part? Witch or wolf?" Tulip asked, shutting the lid of her laptop for once and joining us in the huddle. She and Star were gorgeous. Both blessed with blonde hair and tan-able skin while I looked like Snow White, only lacking the seven dwarfs, summer or winter. *Go figure, and us triplets.*

"Duh! Witch, of course. And it's a period piece, too, so we get to wear *awesome* costumes." Star gave a faux-waltz step, obviously in love with the idea. As the town's resident country and western singer and songwriter to boot, she was into looking good. Sometimes a bit too into it — she attracted more than her fair share of jealous stabs.

"What's it about?" I asked, squinting through the window at a couple who had just appeared walking down the street. They were looking rather chummy, if body language didn't lie. *Is that Constable Ace Collins? With a female?* I slipped on a pair of polar ray sunglasses to sharpen the image.

"A company coming to town to develop a tourist mecca by selling the outside world on the natural hot springs in the area having magical properties."

Hot springs laced with minerals we had for some weird reason, even though Snowy Lake perched on the Canadian Shield. Add in Skull Cave for the wolf clans, and the choice of location was now making a whole lot of sense. I shuddered. Caves gave me the willies. *A nightmare left over from childhood.*

But the sheriff — as I liked to call the constable — and an unknown female? Who was she? Tall and slender with her golden-brown hair tied up in a ponytail, she had the best tan. She also made it easy for the males of the species to appreciate those long, bronzed legs, in her short shorts. Maybe it was time to try the spray tan special that Susie was offering at the Clip Joint this month? My blue-white legs could use some help. *Desperately.*

Star, of course, kept droning on while I sidestepped to the front picture window for the best surveillance. "*And* it's the werewolves' territorial land, while the witches are upset they'll be exposed, so they have to build an alliance to fight the conglomerate. But not everyone's ready for a truce and all kinds of problems develop. It even features the use of arsenic by a suspected serial killer. They've got a poison expert on the set too, the daughter of the actress with the lead role—you know, Mimi Blake. Her daughter knows all about its uses. I forget her name. Oh, they need more billets for some of the extras. Can you think of people who might help with that?"

The pair vanished into Snowy Lake Hardware, with Ace holding the door open with a flourish for Miss Perfect Tan. They shared some comment that made her smile, and possibly giggle—I was too far away to be certain. The hackles on my neck prickled. A light fixture blew out over the first booth in a cascade of exploding sparks. I sighed. Now I'd have to scout the street to find the ladder to change the bulb. Seemed someone was always borrowing the handy-dandy climbing device.

"Sorry, what did you say about a serial killer and arsenic?" I focused on the part of Star's intel that intrigued me.

"Aren't you listening to me? I said a serial killer uses arsenic to kill off characters. Where's your mind this morning?"

Star interrupted her spiel to make a spinning twirl, her usual performance piece when she was over-the-moon excited. The phone rang and I hurried to answer it, hoping it was who I thought it was. *Yes.*

"Auntie T.J. What's the scoop?" I normally had the common sense not to ask, but today was different. I needed intel.

Her voice came over the house phone, all wheezy and breathy. Land lines were the only reliable mode of communication in Snowy Lake, where cell phones were a crap shoot. "Jennifer Morgan. She's a geologist with Altima Explorations. A graduate student from the University of Manitoba. Good grades, though not brilliant. She's here with a small team looking for precious minerals. Mark my word, a big gold strike is imminent. She lives close to his parents' duplex in Winnipeg—did you know they live side by side? Families are old friends. I'm waiting on more information that I should have shortly. I think her father and Ace's mother both work at that virology lab in Winnipeg. Will have verification soon." With that my aunt stopped to take a breath.

I kept a sharp lookout across the street. Fortunately, the telephone rested on the counter near the entrance where we sold all sorts of cookies and bakery goods alongside my favorite magical items, including the new Gilded Tarot by Ciro with its black and gold borders framing lyrical illustrations that whispered to me whenever I ventured nearby. The location was perfect, offering up a proper surveillance position. A stranger came into focus, drawing my full attention—he was so stiff-looking with his pressed beige chino pants, white shirt and black tie and an old-fashioned pocket protector lining up a series of identical pens. He was coming right towards the Tea & Tarot with a determined look on his pasty-white face. His short ginger hair was pressed into service with one section at the crown that wouldn't commit to the status quo sticking up with military defiance.

"I gotta go. Call me later when you know more."

"Roger that. Over and out."

I slipped off the sunglasses just as the angels tinkled a discordant note, announcing the visitor. He gave a harried look around, as though he had no idea how to go about what he needed, but needed it done—and done yesterday.

"Can I help you?" I got to him first. Easy enough, when no one else looked remotely interested.

"Yes, I'm here to check on catering. Do you do that?"

"Catering? Sometimes. What for?"

"I'm with Blue Vest Studios, the company producing the movie *Witches and Wolves*, and we need reliable catering six days a week at the movie set. You know, sandwiches, soups, salads, vegetable trays, desserts, that kind of thing. And especially anything chocolate. Can you do that?" He hurried his words, looking about with eyes that shifted so much I was concerned for his well-being.

"Well, possibly. And we specialize in chocolate, so you're in luck. You must try our death-by-chocolate slice. It's worth dying for with its hooey-gooey center of chocolate ganache and liquid caramel." I caught the gleam in his eye at my description. While I relished the idea of a catering job, I knew most of it would fall to Tulip and me as Star had a role and, no doubt, she'd play that up. Add her bi-weekly singing at the Boots & Lace Tavern and she'd work both excuses for the foreseeable future.

"Would you like to try a sample?" I asked.

"Yes, definitely." The gleam in his eye was blinding now.

I laid a square of the slice on a small plate, added a fork and handed it to him.

He demolished it in two spectacular bites.

"You do love chocolate." I smiled at his satiated expression. Illicit drugs couldn't have given him more

11

of a sense of being in Blissville. "How many people are we talking about?"

"About a hundred and fifty."

"A hundred and fifty meals a day?" My horror must have shown on my face, because he twitched and his eyes spun around like cartwheels.

"Yes, but just simple meals. Nothing fancy. And we'd pay ten dollars a head. One meal will suffice, delivered around noon. Send enough and we can eat off the buffet for the rest of the day. We have refrigerators in most of the trailers. What do you say?"

Hmm. Ten dollars a head times one hundred and fifty meals. Sweet. But I would need to hire an extra hand or two. No way could we manage all that on top of our usual workload. I made some swift calculations.

"Make that eleven dollars a meal and we have a deal."

"Ten dollars and twenty-five cents. Then we have a deal. I'm Howard Smith, by the way, the resident accountant."

"Charm McCall. Ten-fifty. And I'll even throw in our gluten-free dessert, Cake of a Thousand Faces." The yummy cake was called by that quirky name because it could be dolled up any number of ways—its vanilla flavor went with just about everything else in existence. That, and we loved weird names that made people stand up and take notice. "A house speciality that substitutes almond meal for pastry flour. So, as long as the customer is not allergic to nuts, it works really well. Low-carb, high protein."

"Nice. Okay, that'll work," he agreed with a curt nod.

I sucked up losing the extra fifty cents and nodded my acceptance. An accountant would be concerned about costs. I got that, being the one and only bookkeeper for our small business. Cutting costs was essential to survival. Still, it rankled. We'd do the town proud with our catering—I'd make sure of that—even if it ate into profits.

He stuck out his hand for a shake and I was blessed with the dampest paw on the planet, accompanied by a zinger of an image. Howard cared about every penny because he was embezzling company funds, meaning there would be less to steal if I made a decent profit. Sometimes I wished Granny Toogood hadn't banned swearing—I had a few apt descriptors for this weaselly dealer. I also hoped she was feeling better. The doctor had advised a few days of rest and that had me worried.

Instead, I narrowed my eyes at him and he slid his hand from mine. Yuck. I dried my palm by rubbing it discreetly down the side of my jeans, half hidden by my Tea & Tarot apron.

"Can you start tomorrow?" he asked, his desperation leaking through, making his face shiny with sweat. *Probably because the only other quote he most likely got today far exceeded ours. Guaranteed.* The Husky Service on the highway did some catering, but they didn't come cheap. And their bakery goods came out of pre-frozen tubs and boxes. We prided ourselves on everything fresh baked, from scratch—my fingernails were reduced to rubble from constant work. *Proof positive.*

"Tomorrow! So soon?" All the nerves in my body slammed into high gear. There was so much to do to prepare for such a large undertaking. Could it even be done that quickly?

"We'd really appreciate it. Might even find you a bit part in the movie." It wasn't the incentive he expected—I just shook my head, giving his start date some thought. Sometimes it was best to jump into things, otherwise I'd never do it. I just prayed I could pull it off and do my family and our town proud.

"Okay, but minus the movie walk-on."

The relief on his face made me smile, despite his weaselly-ness.

The café door opened abruptly and in strode a young man dressed in expensive dark-wash jeans and a tight black T-shirt clothing a wiry, thin body, his face a study in annoyance. "Howard, I need to speak with you *right now*. Don't think you can just get up and walk out on me, mister." His hand on his hip pressed his case.

Howard's face darkened to a dull red. "Chace, this is not the time or the place. *Go*. I'll catch up with you later."

The man looked as though he was going to object before he about-faced and left. His one-finger salute, reflected in the front window before he pranced away, was not in the best taste. *Hmm*. Good thing Granny wasn't around to cut him down to size. In the nicest, politest way of course — she could make the worst villain tippy-toe around her. *Probably ask him if he needs the finger for anything other than being rude.*

"Please excuse my friend. He's not himself today."

"Oh, who is he then?"

Howard gave me a blank stare.

Baby Ling Ling sauntered in, grabbing my attention as she always announced her arrival with a loud greeting, or warning, depending on how her day was going. Our spectacular white Himalayan with her adorable squished-in face and apricot-colored ears, fluffy tail raised high, proceeded to choose her steps with the utmost care across the tiled floor of the café. I'd guess it was in case we'd had the bad manners to add a trap door since yesterday's saunter. She deigned to notice the new visitor, striding over and giving him a quick sniff. She jumped a couple of feet in the air with a loud howl, her fluffy white fur standing straight on end as though she'd placed her paw on an electrical charge.

"*Hiss.*" She made herself as big as a tiny eight-pound cat could make herself, arched her back and continued the hissing.

"Nice cat," Howard deadpanned.

"Careful what you say to her. Ling Ling's officially multi-lingual since our librarian, Miriam, added Portuguese to her weekly slate of free language lessons." I just couldn't resist, not liking his look of disdain. Or his cheapness that was certain to affect our bottom line.

His look of confusion was quite satisfying. He gave Ling Ling a wide berth and headed for the door.

"Okay, then, we'll expect you tomorrow? You'll get paid once a week, just come by my office and I'll cut you a check. Oh, and the camp's out by Spirit Springs." He paused, his hand on the doorknob, obviously needing confirmation.

"Yes, I know where the camp is, and the food will be there. You can count on the McCall family. We never go back on our word." I gave him a level look that he declined to return. A nervous twitch of his nose and he hopped out of the café.

"That guy has a blackish aura with streaks of gray," Tulip said, pursing her lips.

"Yeah, no surprise—he's working under a brain cloud." I didn't want to say the words *embezzling cocaine addict* out loud and sink the project before it started. "And since when did you start seeing auras?" And what was I going to do with the unwanted knowledge that the guy was stealing company funds? *A moral dilemma.* I shouldn't think that was business as normal, even for the movie industry.

She gave me a smug look. "You're not the only one discovering gifts since we turned twenty-one on July first."

"Nice. Hey, what color's mine?"

"Depends."

"What do you mean?"

"It's usually light with a halo of pink, silver or gold, but right now it's tinged with green. Never seen that color on you before. Interesting."

Movement across the street drew my attention, and out of Snowy Lake Hardware popped Ace and his fancy friend. Hmm. She was swinging that ponytail so much it was in peril of getting caught in something. *Not that that would be a bad thing.* I envisioned it catching in the closing door and...

"Who's that with Ace?" Tulip joined me at the window. "By the way, your aura's getting greener. Maybe you're jealous, eh?" She poked me with a sharp elbow.

"Ow! I'm not jealous. That's Jennifer Morgan, an old family friend of Ace's. Graduate student here on geology exploration," I said through clenched teeth. What else was going on? She lightly swatted Ace's arm in feigned anger play, making me wince. *A flirt to boot.*

They crossed the street and strolled merrily toward the café. I ducked out of the window and hurried to continue dusting the shelves. Tulip dallied.

"Move away from there, they'll see you spying on them," I hissed at her.

"So?" She shrugged, but thankfully moved toward her laptop again and got back to keyboarding. *Good, just write the blog already and pretend nothing's going on.* And what exactly *was* going on?

The angel chimes sang out the new arrivals with all the enthusiasm of a Baptist congregation. *I swear they know more about who's coming into our café than I do, changing their mood with each customer they announce.*

"Mornin', Charm, Tulip. I'd like you to meet an old family friend, Jennifer Morgan," Ace said with a respectful tilt of his impressive hat. Star had long vanished into the back recesses of the kitchen, probably to text or call everyone of the Northern Lights Coven about her shiny new job. I sighed. *Shoot.* I had to get to the Grab-n-go and buy supplies for tomorrow's catering or I'd be sunk.

I gave the pair a quick greeting, unable to keep from noticing how sweet-smelling our almost-brand-new Mountie was that morning. The fragrance of soap and a special mix that was all Ace's own rolled off him in waves, like pheromones at a picnic. If I was an ant, I'd be crawling all over him. I took a deep appreciative breath, remembering to give the new female a smile of welcome. If Granny Toogood heard that I'd lost my manners, well, suffice to say, there would be repercussions. Three things she can't abide, that special woman who took us in at the age of eight when we arrived unannounced on her doorstep — swearing, speaking ill of the dead and sex talk. But politeness, that was a given. Ace himself was no slouch in that department either, having grown up in the southern state of Kentucky before his parents moved with their three sons to Canada.

"What are you doing in Snowy Lake, Jennifer?" I asked, though it was a useless waste of time to confirm my aunt's information. She was always spot on. We all have our gifts in Snowy Lake. Mine is finding lost objects and a recent development I hadn't quite worked my mind around yet — some kind of weird ability to heal the human body—while Auntie T.J.'s was always knowing the news first.

"I'm a graduate student from the University of Manitoba. We're working with Altima Explorations, checking for alluvial gold deposits." Her voice had a serious edge to it, mixed with a lyrical quality.

"Ah, the kind deposited through water movements. But, of course, the best indicator is the fact that substantial gold deposits were found here in the past," I added, entirely grateful for my need to know a little something about everything, when her eyes lit up with interest.

"Charm's a major league bookworm," Ace said with an appreciative smile.

Great. I'd just placed myself into the boring-librarian category. Maybe it was time for dark-framed glasses. *Nah, I don't even wear contacts. I'm one of the lucky ones, so far. Never been sick one day in my life, touch wood. Annoys my sisters no end when they're stricken by a runny nose or fever.*

"She's a lot more than that, Ace. She runs a business and still manages to look gorgeous."

Oh no. She didn't just say that. The. Worst. Possible. Thing. A woman who looked like she did and was super-nice to other women? My barely begun romance was dead in the water. *Kaput.* All Ace and I had shared was one kiss, though. I sighed. *But what a kiss.* A treasured memory now, since it didn't look like any more would be forthcoming. It didn't help that Tulip made a circle with her forefinger and thumb at me, a gesture meant to emphasize my aura getting greener, no doubt.

A horrendous sound struck my brain. *Oh, jeez, not today.*

"Who's that?" Jennifer pointed out of the window, her eyes wide open.

I cringed. Auntie T.J., in full battle dress and playing bagpipes usually reserved for fending off bear attacks, marched by the café's entrance. At least the residents would turn a blind eye, knowing my family, though my auntie didn't make it easy wearing head-to-toe plaid.

"That's my auntie. She's—uh—driving away evil spirits. Just ignore her. So, what can I do for you this morning? Quiche? Coffee?" I asked brightly, pretending it was business as usual. "We make mini-breakfast quiches in pastry pockets, easy for our customers to take to go." I pointed them out to Jennifer. "How about you, Constable?"

"Sorry, no time, today, darlin'. I'm heading out to check that new movie set, to make sure everything's up to code," Ace said.

Jennifer's eyebrows rose at the casual "darlin'", but she continued to smile like a sunny pixie. At least her lips did. Her eyeballs appeared frozen over. "And I've got to get to work. Ace helped me pick up some supplies." She held up the small Snowy Lake Hardware bag she was carrying as proof of their prior engagement.

"Maybe a croissant or a cheese scone?" For some reason I couldn't let it go. She looked a tad narrow in the hips.

"Oh, do you make cheese scones?" she squealed. "My grandmother always did when we visited the farm each summer vacation. I love them!"

I inwardly groaned. *Great, now I've made the elder woman category.* "Yes, it's an old family recipe of Granny Toogood."

"Granny Toogood?" she inquired, turning to check out our glass display of bakery goods with a keen interest.

"You'll meet her soon. She's the matriarch of our family."

"I do believe I must try them." She pointed at a peanut butter cookie tray lined up with all the other array of choices. "And one of those as well."

"Ace?" I asked, giving him a wee nudge, making sure to use his first name this time.

"Nothing for me, thanks." Well, that was a first. What was the deal? *Suddenly watching your weight, big guy? No need for that, no sir, not with that lean six-pack, quarterback shoulders and thighs like a lumberjack who's been cutting down trees all day. Oh my…*

"Don't worry. We haven't laced anything with cyanide this week," I teased, filling the silence. "Besides, champagne works best." He'd get the tribute to Agatha Christie's *Sparkling Cyanide* and our last case where the murderess had placed the poison in our apricot jam. *The nerve of the banker's wife, making our wares suspect.*

"That's good to know," Ace deadpanned, though he gave me a wink. *Nice.*

Jennifer opened the blue and white starred bakery bag I handed her with its Tea & Tarot moniker designed by Tulip, diving into the cheddar cheese scone. "Oh, this is wonderful. So moist. Ace, you must try a bite." She didn't wait for an answer, but force-fed him. He accepted the morsel from her fingers, swallowing it. She turned to give me a sly victory grin.

My heart sank.

Chapter Two

"It was lovely to meet you, Charm," she said. *Yeah, right.*

I held out my hand for a shake, making her swallow the last of the scone in a hurry to reciprocate. I held on to her fingers for a few extra seconds, hoping to pick up vibrations or an image. *Oh yeah, not so nice at all.*

She narrowed her eyes at me, tugging her hand away. "What do I owe you?"

"Think of it as a 'welcome to our town' present. No need to pay." I brushed her off.

"I don't remember getting any treats for free," Ace said with a pretend frown.

"No?" I asked with a smug smile. "Have you forgotten the special one we shared in back?"

His lips pursed and he tipped his hat. "No, I could never forget that."

My peripheral vison caught a glimpse of Jennifer looking from Ace to me while he and I continued to lock glances. My knees began to weaken under the scrutiny of his hot gaze, making me forget we had an audience. Ace had a way of making time stand still and every other activity become a blur around us.

"Well, we should be going," she ventured, tugging at his arm, drawing my fuzzy attention. Ace has the most amazing, expressive eyes. A woman could get lost in them if she wasn't careful. "I promised my prof I'd be back soon as possible."

Ace leaned down to speak close in my ear to avoid being overheard, ignoring his guest. His breath flowed against the side of my neck, eliciting a caress of warm tingles and shivers down my body. "Don't be mentioning that amazing kiss if you don't expect me to be back for seconds. I'll see you later, darlin'."

I swallowed, nodding my head. "Yes, later, please."

"You can count on it. Oh, and I wanted to drop off a book I just finished reading, *Real Magic* by Dean Radin, PhD. I think you'll enjoy it. He discusses the secret power of the universe. One particular section on blessing food, specifically chocolate, where he talks about belief becoming biology should interest you."

"Thanks, I do have a thing about food being best when blessed, rhyming intended." I grinned. "And I've got one for you too. *E-squared* by Pam Grout. You'll like it. It's about how thoughts create reality. I know how much you love control, Constable." I gave him my best smile.

He nodded, tipping his awesome hat with an effortless flick of his fingers.

"Oh, and, Jennifer..." I had a sudden inspiration for a parting zinger. "There's been *eluvial* gold deposits found hereabouts on occasion. You know, just in case that helps your team in some small way." I added an innocent grin.

With a curt nod, Jennifer finally managed to tug Ace out of the door, the angel chimes making a chorus of excited squeals when the door slammed shut behind her highness. Maybe from the high level of communication Ace and I had just shared? Or, more likely, because she didn't enjoy it nearly as much as the two of us had.

"Jennifer seemed very sweet," Tulip said, looking up from her laptop, her blue eyes filled with innocence. Was she being facetious? If she could see auras, she had to know something was up.

"Yeah, sure. As sweet as a gunny sack of hissing vipers," I muttered under my breath.

Of course, Tulip hadn't been party to what I had just glimpsed. Jennifer wasn't just here for the dig — she was here to win Ace, and she saw me as the rival to beat. Well, no McCall backed down from a challenge, unless she was dead, a goner, deceased, no more. We hadn't survived being unceremoniously dumped at Granny Toogood's when we were eight to take any flack from anyone now. I ignored the doubts that bubbled to the surface, insisting that we'd been thrown away once like garbage, what was to stop it happening again?

"Oh shoot, look at the time. I gotta go." I tore off my apron that I wore over my white T-shirt and jeans, intent on heading to the Grab-n-go. *Everyone's plagued by something from their past, right? Why should I be treated as special?* "Can you hold the fort?" I asked Tulip.

"Sure."

I raced through the café and into the kitchen. And there was Star still on her phone. She didn't look up but continued texting. *Natch.*

"Our turn to host the coven tomorrow," she said, still staring at her phone, thumbs flying. Star had better luck with cell phone service than anyone else in town. What was her secret?

I groaned. Loudly. I loved spending time with my favorite women, but time was going to be tighter than ever. "Darn, our turn so soon? I've just taken on a *huge* catering contract for the movie set. We have to hire someone else. ASAP. Any suggestions? Any of your friends need a job for a few weeks?" I could ask our scary Russian boarder, Ivana Petro, who occupied the suite upstairs across from mine, but being forced into the same confining kitchen with her for days on end? *Oh boy. She's a tad sensitive. And, did I mention, very, very scary?*

"I volunteered us because Christine canceled — she's sick." She shrugged. "Wouldn't say what it was. She sounded awful. And yeah, I think James Watson's looking for work. His mother is ready to throw him out of the basement. Another failure to launch."

"A guy? I was thinking someone female." I didn't have anything against the guy, just the idea had never occurred to me before.

"What?" She looked up from her phone. "You think the male of the species can't cook and bake? And you did say you're desperate. You know, I'll be too busy with the movie role and singing at the Boots & Lace to be of much help here."

Well played. I groaned. "Okay, okay, call him. And ask if he can start today? I'll be back with supplies in a jiff."

"That reminds me, it's not long until pot becomes legal. I think it's time we amped up a few recipes. Maybe James can stay on and help with that after the movie finishes? Tulip and I have some wonderful ideas to make tons of money by getting into the business pronto." She waggled her eyebrows at me, enjoying my obvious discomfort about the proposition.

Sure, I'd had a change of heart with what I knew about the substance now. I mean, Granny used it for her arthritis, but still, I had misgivings.

"And the lure would help me persuade James to take the job *and* help pay his salary this fall."

"Let's not get ahead of ourselves. And you're in charge of snacks for tomorrow. Either that, or you need to cancel. I can't do everything around here."

She blessed me by making a face. "Okay, it's on me. But don't be such a stick in the mud. I swear to take care of it." She stopped to make a cross over her heart, then added with a full-on grin, "*Potcakes that sell like hotcakes. You have my personal guarantee for that one.*"

I shook my head, but couldn't hide a grin. *Star, the incorrigible triplet.*

"Just call him. And get busy on treats for the coven. *Anything* chocolate will do."

"Duh."

I exited the café, dashing into the back alley where I'd parked Thor, my faithful old Cherokee Jeep. I'd bought him off an old trapper for a free breakfast quiche every day for a year. The barter system was a thing of beauty in small town Canada where self-reliance was an essential virtue of survival.

I drove Thor the three blocks to the Grab-n-go and parked in front of the brightly lit grocery store that doubled as the liquor commission and lottery center. *One-stop shopping.*

I grabbed a grocery cart and made a beeline for the produce section. I was just bundling up bunches of romaine lettuce when the sound of bottles clanking together drew my attention to the liquor area across the aisle. A short man with a thick black mustache and swarthy complexion was busy filling up his basket with a large assortment of high-end liquor. Dressed in a dark shirt, dress pants with shiny shoes and a wide black tie, he looked like most everyone's idea of an archetypical hitman. If I ever got some of my ideas on paper for a murder mystery, he'd have a huge role to play. *Mafia.* He glanced my way, his dark, intense look almost chilling. *Oh yeah. Definitely.*

I nodded pleasantly. He returned my greeting with a smirk, a wink and a nod, then returned to his business. *Okay, bit over-played.* I got down to filling my cart, Mafia Guy soon forgotten with my personal need to out-race time.

At the till, I paid for my purchases, then pushed the cart through the automatic door and into the parking lot. The handle of the cart was beyond sticky, and I wiped my hands on my jeans with disgust. Soon as I got back in Thor, I'd be using a slew of disinfectant wipes. I was loading the numerous bags onto the back seat when the sound of a throat being cleared made me look up. Not far as it happened, my interrupter being as height-challenged as I was.

Oh shoot, Mafia Guy was standing too close with a fancy leer pasted on his swarthy face, and the man must have been forty if he was a day. *And make that a well-lived forty.*

"Hello, I'm Guido Morello, at your service. I noticed you watching me in the store and I thought I should introduce myself."

"Uh-huh." I didn't offer my name, not wanting to encourage the guy.

"And what's your name, pretty lady?"

Figures. He had a distinct Boston accent, with no apparent use for the consonant *r*. They even have a term for it in Bean Town USA, the No R lifestyle. He certainly had the swagger down pat, thumbs hooked in his leather belt loops.

"I'm Charm McCall. We run the Tea & Tarot café. I'm sorry, I have to go. Just got a big catering contract and I'm running late."

"Ah-ha." He'd spoken like he'd just discovered the mystery of the builders of the pyramids. "You must be the person Howard Smith hired to cater for our film set. Nice. Looks like we'll be seeing *lots* of each other. Howard's married to my cousin, by the way—we're tight." He held up two crossed fingers in case I didn't get it.

"Hang dai?" I joked, making reference to a similar scene in *Deadwood* when Wu, the Chinese top dog, acknowledges Al Swearingen's help by calling them brothers. Of course, the reference went right over the mob guy's head. And what was I doing, encouraging this particular conversation? I mentally swatted myself.

He scratched his head, not disturbing one hair of his precise tinted-black pompadour in the process. "Sorry, not getting it."

"My bad. Good to know about your marriage to Howard Smith's cousin, though. Now, if you'll excuse me, I *really* have to go."

"No, no, *not* me. I'm not married. Howard's married to *my* cousin." He chuckled as though it was the funniest thing ever and probably thought it explained my reluctance to talk further. Great, I really did need my head examined.

"Yes, well, I'm sure we'll meet up again on set."

"You can bet on it, pretty lady, I'll be keeping my eye out for you. You do stand out in Snowtown."

"Snowy Lake," I corrected. *Yup. It's official. I'm the best at giving false positives to strangers when I should be returning zipola, nothing, nada.* I gave him a quick nod and jumped back into Thor. I raced to the café, hovering at the speed limit. Ace had decided to clean up bad driving habits in town and he had his hands full, since making U-turns on Main Street was a traditional practice. I didn't want the embarrassment of being stopped by him. *Again.*

I unloaded supplies, carting the heavy bags in the back door and plunking them on the kitchen counter. Star was now nowhere to be seen, but there was a note scrawled on the erasable whiteboard.

Expect James at eleven.

I glanced at the rooster clock. *Great.* He'd be here in an hour. The phone rang and I waited for someone out front to answer it, being rather busy chopping vegetables and keeping an eye on the chicken breasts baking in the oven.

"Charm, it's for you," Tulip shouted from the front, making me wince.

Drying my hands on a towel, I picked up the phone.

"Charm?" Christine Blackmore asked, her voice thickened by emotion. She'd been crying. My heart squeezed in sympathy.

"Hi, Christine. Sorry you're not feeling well. Anything I can do?" This was not a cold or the flu my new friend was suffering from — and a person wouldn't have to be psychic to pick that up. She was acutely depressed. I prayed it wasn't what I suspected.

"Yes, actually, there is something." She hesitated, her tone uncertain. "I heard what you did for Helen and Elsie and I was wondering — could you help me? Heal my problem?" She didn't even want to call it by its real name. *Infertility.* "I'm so upset I don't know what to do." Helen Davis had cancer, or at least *had* had it, according to her doctors. When I'd been working on the list of suspects for the murder of Mrs. Hurst and the

28

poisoned apricot jam fiasco, I had spent a fateful, enlightening afternoon with Helen. Then I'd helped her friend Elsie when she'd asked me to try. Whether the healing was permanent or not for the two of them remained to be seen. As Granny liked to say, '*Things are never as bad as you think they are, or as good as you want them to be.*'

"Christine, I don't know —"

"I have nowhere else to turn, no one else to ask. Please, Charm, could we just give it a try? Just one time?" The desperation in her tone touched my heart again. Her problem of infertility threatened the very foundations of her marriage to Sean, a definite rascal and my number-one suspect in the recent murder investigation. He wanted a son. *Yesterday.*

"Okay. But I can't promise anything. I have no idea how it works, or if I can help with your problem." I sighed. Was I doing the right thing or just raising false hope? If it turned out to be the latter, I'd never forgive myself.

"No worries. I would never hold you responsible if it doesn't go well. I'm the one asking for your help. Thanks, Charm. Can we try today?"

"Oh, I don't know. I just took on a *huge* catering contract and I have someone I need to train —"

"I can help you with that! I'll send over our new housekeeper, Suzanna. She can give you a hand, at least until you get back to the café. Longer, if you need her. Heck, if you can help me, I'll offer you her services, pre-paid till Christmas at least."

Her voice had brightened considerably with raw hope. My resistance vanished. Someone needed my help. And I could always work all night if I had to. It wasn't as though I hadn't done that before. Gosh, how many times had I prayed for a clone? A nice strong clone who enjoyed taking orders from me and never balked at chores.

"Okay, sure. I'll be right over. Just got to take the chicken out of the oven."

"Thanks. You're the best."

"Please, don't get your hopes up too much. I don't know how much help—"

But she had already hung up.

The goddess doesn't give you more than you can handle, right? Hmm, well, right then, I needed the help of every goddess that had ever lived. Anywhere.

Chapter Three

I parked Thor in Christine's driveway, noting the house's pulled drapes. Depression hung over the house like a rain cloud. I sent a quick appeal into the universe — *Please let me help Christine.*

After striding with determination toward the front door, I rang the doorbell, listening to it echo throughout the Blackmores' abode. The door opened abruptly, my new friend obviously having been hovering nearby. The look of hope she was working hard to supress sent a sharp arrow of empathy straight through me.

"Thanks for coming. Please, please come in. Can I get you anything? Tea? Coffee? A drink? Something to eat? I have tons of choices." Her words tumbled over each other while she led the way inside her spacious home, down the hallway to the kitchen outfitted with fancy chrome appliances. Christine had money, being a former Davis, but needed something cash couldn't buy. *Happiness.*

"Water's fine."

I checked her out while I pulled a bar stool away from under the kitchen island and jumped aboard. She was rummaging in the frig, hauling out two bottled waters. Even in her depression she had made the effort to comb her mahogany-colored hair and apply makeup to her Restylane-assisted face, though she hadn't managed to hide all traces of her recent crying jag, which had probably been on account of her husband, Sean, the reason she was so desperate to keep up appearances. It shouldn't have been like that.

"Are you sure about all this, Christine? I mean, if a man loves you…"

She plunked the water bottles down on the island in front of us, choosing a seat beside me. "Completely and utterly sure. I want a child of my own more than you can know. It's all I've dreamed of for years, holding my own baby in my arms. This is *not* just about Sean, though heaven knows he wants a child as much as I do."

"Okay." I nodded, twisting the cap on the plastic bottle to open it. "I'll try." I took a sip of water.

"Thanks, Charm. I knew you wouldn't let me down." Her expectant expression further bruised my heart. This had all kinds of weirdness attached, considering a few weeks ago we'd had very little to say to each other, both thinking we had nothing in common. *Turns out everybody has something in common.* Well, except for serial killers. They were still the monsters among us.

"Shall we start?" I asked, the kitchen clock ticking in the background a constant reminder of how much I had to do today, tomorrow, next week…

"Sure." She held her hands out to me and I covered them with mine. "What do you want me to think about?"

"Just relax. Maybe think about having a baby," I suggested, really not sure of what would work best, this being only my third time to try this. In a normal lost-item-reading, of which I've done a gazillion, I asked a customer to just think about the lost treasure, recall when they'd last seen it.

I closed my eyes. As with Helen Davis and her friend Elsie, I was taken inside her body, finding myself traveling down veins and artery pathways, past glistening organs to a central location in her belly. Her uterus, it had to be. It looked nice and pink, a cozy home. But as I wandered around the space, a tube branching off from the organ appeared, dark and solid, plugged with tissue. It screamed *invader*.

I attacked it with all my being, sending a death ray like in a video game. Awesome energy flowed through me, exploding from somewhere deep inside. The evil plug turned a bright red hue, lit up with a huge charge of electricity. I focused as hard as I could on the villain, wanting to drive it out. To blow it to pieces, grab a hold of it and force it to leave, all the while thinking I had done this before, a very long time ago in a place far, far away...

My hands remained electrified and clutching Christine's while I envisioned her fallopian tube back to a healthy pink, all remnants of the blockage blasted to smithereens. Then I went looking for the other tube, because surely it was plausible, if she couldn't get pregnant, there could be a second plug? There was. And I went into my avenger mode again. The second tube looking normal, I slumped back onto the stool. I had done all I could. A wave of dizziness overcame me, and I grabbed for the water bottle, gulping half of it down in mere seconds.

"Did it work, Charm? Do you think so?"

I gave her a weak smile, my body trembling from fatigue, tears blurring my vision. This healing business was a minefield of emotion. I wanted a guarantee that did not exist—Christine having a healthy child to love.

"Maybe. I don't know for sure."

"What did you see?"

"I think your fallopian tubes were blocked. I tried to blast the debris away. They look better, pinker. I truly hope it makes a difference, Christine." I sat still, waiting for the white pinpricks of light dancing across my vision to disappear before I got up to leave.

"That's what the doctor said was wrong and not fixable—too much scar tissue. I have a good feeling about this." She gave me a glance. "You look a bit peaked, Charm. Would you like something to eat? I have fruit salad all made up."

"You know, yes, I could use something with a bit of natural sugar and chock full of vitamins." I gave her a wan smile, the pesky low blood pressure still plaguing me.

She got up—she looked energized at least—and grabbed a bowl of colorful fruit from the shiny new aluminum frig. I couldn't imagine keeping fingerprints off that human energy sucker. The fruit helped me and I relished the freshness down to the last bite. "Thanks, I needed that." I set the engraved teaspoon on the napkin beside the placemat.

"I can't thank you enough. Even if it doesn't work, I know you tried your best."

I leaned forward and we hugged. "I hope it works, goddess willing."

She brushed a few tears away, giving me the bravest smile.

A last hug at the front door and I jogged down the driveway and jumped into Thor. I gunned the motor and set off.

The sounds of a siren pierced my frantic brain. *No!* I glanced in the rear-view mirror. *Shoot. Constable Ace.* I eased my heavy foot off the gas petal and directed the Jeep to the curb. I sat, banging my head on the steering wheel when the expected knock came on the glass. I glanced over, then rolled the window down.

"You should be kinder to that noggin of yours," he said, pursing his lips. "Considering your nickname." He stood all tall and righteous by the window, making me twist my neck to see him under the low-hanging clouds.

I groaned. "No, please, *please* don't tell me—"

"Brainiac. Suits you." His scent wafted in the window, further annoying me. Why couldn't I get a handle on this attraction? Not to mention I needed to get to the bottom of this "one true love" rule if I wanted to keep my goddess-given gifts…or so Granny claimed.

"So, who am I going to have to murder for giving up that state secret?" I asked.

"Star did the honors. But I think I have a better nickname in mind for you," he teased.

Intriguing. "What's that?"

"Leadfoot."

I groaned. "No. Not that. If you call me that, I'm going to go back to yours—Bigfoot. Just so you're warned."

"That's Constable Bigfoot to you. No, I think you're much too pretty for that nickname. Though you gave a spectacular impression of Miss Marple during the murder investigation."

"No way! I'm not an old lady with white hair!" Though the truth was I was flattered by the comparison to Agatha Christie's beloved character.

"I'll work on it. Come up with something you might actually like. Now, about your speeding. What's the darn rush, Miss McCall?"

"Why are you back here anyway? I thought you were spending the day with that geologist?" *She who shall remain nameless.*

"Don't change the subject. It just didn't take that long at the movie set, and Jennifer's at another location, working. So, what gives? You've been doing so well, too. Keeping out of police business, watching the speed limit, not pulling illegal U-turns on Main Street." He laid his extra-large hands on the window of my Jeep, leaning down and staring directly into my eyes with those liquid pools this woman just wanted to sink into. *Oh boy.*

"Well, the murder rate's been down for a while, thanks to yours truly, so no police business to interfere with at the moment, and I have been watching my Ps and Qs," I said, unable to keep the snugness from my tone.

"Joke all you like, but if I ever catch you interfering with an official investigation ever again without your name stamped on a police shield, well, suffice to say you might find yourself up the creek without the proverbial paddle."

"I've got my own paddle, thank you very much. I canoe every summer. And you can't deny I helped your investigation, in the end."

He squinted at me, a hint of danger flashing between us. "You'll be lucky if I don't use that paddle on a certain behind. License and registration," he said, the deep timbre of his voice making my body hum.

"Are you threatening me, Officer?" Self-righteous anger bubbled to the surface. Why did I let this man pull my strings? I just couldn't seem to help myself, pleading the Fifth Amendment. Or was that just the case in the United States? Heck, the Canadian Charter of Rights and Freedoms must protect us just as well. *I should check that out.*

"Never," he said, a smile quirking the edges of his mouth. He took the registration papers for Thor and my license card from my hands and gave them a cursory glance. "Not when there are so many other things I'd much rather do with you."

"Oh really?" This was even more intriguing than a new nickname. "Pray tell."

"Like invite you to dinner tonight. My place. Seven o'clock." He handed me back my license and registration without giving me a ticket. *Phew.*

"Oh shoot, I forgot." I remembered the string of jobs I'd just laid out end to end for the foreseeable future. "I'll be pulling an all-nighter. Got a catering contract for the movie. I'll be preparing a hundred and fifty meals a day, six days a week for a while."

He whistled, stepping back from the open window. "I best not keep you then. But the invitation stands. Anytime, darlin'. You still got to eat, right?"

"Don't keep your fingers crossed. But maybe when I get some new help trained, I might make the time for my very own Mr. Bigfoot event." And with that I hit the gas. Then grinned in the rear-view mirror at the picture of Ace standing tall and shaking his forefinger at me.

A few minutes later, I entered the back door of the Tea & Tarot, pondering my recent conversation. I needed to come up with a better nickname for Ace too, one that would grab his attention. Like Top Gun. Or Mr. 44, seeing as how he was always packing. Or the very apt Eye Candy. Nah. Too obvious. How about the Queen's Cowboy, the unofficial title for RCMP officers from way back? That suited. Or Hercules? Maybe. But, most of all, I needed to keep him out of Miss Not-so-nice-at-all's clutches. I sighed. I'd done a spectacular job of driving him away just now. I should have taken him up on dinner. Made the time. And exactly why was I pondering all this when I had a gazillion things to do? That Mountie drove me freakin' crazy.

I groaned, taking in the piles of foodstuffs laid out on the counter and requiring immediate attention. Not another soul in sight. And where exactly was my promised new helper, James? I sighed, then hurried to wash my hands at the sink, slipped on my apron and got down to the myriad tasks that awaited.

The sound of footfalls hurrying through the café and into the kitchen drew my attention. James Watson appeared in the doorway, looking flustered, his wholesome round face topped by a huge crown of thick brown hair that he kept shaved close at the sides and back. He was wearing a blue and white Jets hockey jersey. He'd been a year ahead of us in school, and I knew his family well. They were hard-working people, so we stood a chance here. I checked the clock — twelve-thirty, making him an hour and a half late. Even his adorable puppy-dog eyes weren't going to be of much help.

I gave him a silent stare, waiting for an explanation.

"Oh, gosh, I'm so sorry, Charm! I would have been on time, but Star needed my help."

"Oh really." I couldn't keep the edge out of my tone, more annoyed by my sister than anything else. "Doing what, pray tell?"

He blushed, obviously nervous. Sympathy welled up, but I forced it down. I had to set the tone now or this would not work out. I needed help I could count on. The next few weeks were going to be insane.

"Star asked me to practice her lines with her. You know, she's in the movie, *Witches and Wolves*! But, of course, she would be, right! She's so beautiful and talented. Oh, I mean, you're all so beautiful —"

"I see. Perhaps the two of you could arrange to do that *after* all the work is completed?"

"Oh, yes, of course. It won't happen again, I promise. And I'll stay as long as it takes. Don't even worry about the overtime. I want to make it up to you."

My resolve softened with his earnestness. Guys could be so easily led astray by my thoughtless sister. "No worries. Let's just get at it. I'll have a word with Star." An idea came to me about how to get the better of a certain Mountie. "Say, your brother casts in metals, right?"

"Yeah, Alex does. Why? You got a project in mind? We'd give you the family rate," he promised. "Maybe make up for my tardiness."

"No need. I'll pay what's fair." I explained what I had in mind, even doing a quick spontaneous sketch.

"Are you sure it's legal?"

I shrugged. "Why not? I was pretty much given permission by our new Mountie anyway. The idea came from him."

"Oh yeah, figures. He has a thing for you. Whole town's talking about it."

I blushed so red my ears felt on fire. "Ah, I think we'd best get down to work now."

"Good idea. I'll pass on your request to my brother later. It shouldn't take him very long, a day or two. What do you want me to do first?"

"Let's see. We need to prepare food for one hundred and fifty people by noon tomorrow with loads of extras for everyone to munch on all day, so more like two hundred meals in total." I ticked things off on my fingers. "The veggies need chopping, the salad greens washed, the meat and cheese sliced, the desserts assembled, buns baked." I stopped for a moment to think of the ideal battle plan. *Best to wait to bake the buns in the morning to make sure they're fresh.* "I'll work on desserts if you'd like to start with vegetable prep?"

"Sure, whatever you need." A broad smile accompanied James' words and we settled down to work. *Fingers crossed that we can find our rhythm.*

When Suzanna arrived a few minutes later, she scoped out the situation and, without being told what to do, just got on with it. *Hey, this just might work out after all.*

I popped the second batch of death-by-chocolate slice into the oven and straightened, rubbing my lower back. Six-thirty. There was still a lot to do, but we had a real handle on it now. I gave my crew a thumbs-up, congratulating myself on what might be a win-win.

Stiletto heels clicked sharply on tile. I stood straighter. *Ivana Petrov.* No one else wore shoes that literally drilled holes in the floor. *Note to self — Buy more floor putty next trip to Snowy Lake Hardware, and never think win-win.* I might have jinxed things. When our boarder was on the war path, the floors took a heck of a beating. *Hmm.* Ivana, with her bright red Medusa hair and steely gray eyes, would have a lot in common with that guy I met at the Grab-n-go, Guido Morello. Did the Russian Bratva mix with the Mafia? Or were they eternal enemies like lions and hyenas? I loved my nature shows.

Ivana came into view, the expression on her gorgeous face wild. I froze. She was breathing hard, making her spectacular rack move up and down in her low-cut top, threatening full exposure of her assets. It had happened a time or two, and she'd just calmly tucked her bosom back in place. *Nerves of steel.* I glanced over at James to see how he was faring. He had also stopped dead, his hand poised with a sharp knife over the cutting board. I sent up a quick protection spell. The last thing I needed was him cutting off a finger.

My throat dry, I croaked out a few words. "Ivana, how lovely to see you."

"I have best news." She pressed a fist to her breast about where her heart should have been, accompanied by an adoring look.

I let out a deep breath. "Good. Glad to hear it." For once I wasn't being taken to task for some imagined slight. She had a few quirks, one being I had to be the one to personally invite her to any event, even if it was assumed that the whole town would be there.

She waited, eyebrows raised.

"Ahh, please, won't you share the good news with your friends?" I gave a nod of respect, adding a wide gesture with my hand that included my new crew. Suzanna was less impressed by the interruption, still busy assembling mini-quiches, though on closer inspection she'd gone rather pale. Well, at least James wasn't harming himself by not moving.

"We bunk now. Bosom buddies."

"Sorry, bunk? Not catching your drift."

"We sleep same bed."

"I have a bed. A perfectly good bed." Mystified, I waited for an explanation.

"I think Ivana means that the movie crew are looking for billets for some of their people. You know, like when hockey players come to town and anyone with an extra bedroom puts them up for the tournament, gratis," Suzanna said.

"Oh, they don't have enough trailers for everyone?" The light went on. Hadn't Star said something about it

41

earlier when I had been a tad distracted? I shook my head vigorously as the scariest thought in the world came on board. "No, absolutely not! I'm not letting out my suite to someone! They can't be that short of beds that they need mine. Isn't it enough that I'm going to be up cooking and baking till all hours? I'm not going to be chased out of my own bed, too."

Ivana blinked. Her lips pursed, her eyes shooting daggers. Really. I could feel them hit numerous places on my body. "Charm not happy with Ivana."

"No, no, it's *nothing* like that. I swear. I'm *very* happy with Ivana. But this is all a bit sudden—"

She gave a nod of total satisfaction. "I tell them Ivana and Charm bunk together." She spun around and marched out of the room.

"Ivana, no, please!" I raced to stop her and face-planted on the floor, tripping over my own darn feet.

Chapter Four

James, being the closest, rushed to my aid. He held out his hands, giving me a boost up from the floor.

"Should have used a protection spell for myself," I muttered, checking if my nose still faced forward. It did.

"You're so good at magic. Why don't you cast some kind of a ward-like spell and keep Ivana at a safe distance? The whole town would appreciate it." He gave me a speculative look, his hazel eyes gleaming with interest. He really had embraced his family's work ethic. We'd achieved more than I had expected in record time, putting my sisters to shame. *Good on him.*

"Nah, I can't do that." Though I had to privately admit I had been sorely tempted on occasion. "I only seem to be able to produce white magic. Black magic eludes me. So, I guess I've got a new roommate." Visions of the Russian mob invading Ivana's suite terrified me. It was a real possibility.

The back door must have opened during the fiasco, because there stood the Queen's own cowboy, carrying a picnic basket. I've always had a hankering for a man riding free on the range, a sturdy horse supporting his hot bod.

He looked from James to me, confusion furrowing his brow.

"Hey, cowboy," I said, trying it out.

"Miss McCall."

My turn to frown at the cold chill of his tone. What did he have against cowboys, for heaven's sake?

"I brought you something to eat, but I can see you're busy..." He gave a curt nod at James, plunked the basket down on the nearest counter and spun on his heels.

"No, wait, let's eat together!" Too late. He'd already vanished through the back door. What was his problem? I could make some time now that I had acquired two fabulous kitchen genii to watch my back.

"I'd better get back to work." James moved away, picking up the chopping knife. He began slicing the rest of the vegetables into bite-sized pieces. I went over to the basket and opened the lid, curious to check out what Ace had chosen for our supper. *Oh*, very nice. Sliced pepper steak, potato salad and French bread with two generous portions of chocolate cake and thick buttercream icing made my mouth water. Why had he gone to all this trouble then vanished? I shook my head. *Shame to let it go to waste.* I dived right in. Dessert first — life was too short to take unnecessary chances.

"Just saw our sheriff driving down the street and his aura's gone all kerflooey. Bright red and green fireworks streaking in every direction when it's normally a nice steady true-blue. What did you do to the poor guy?" Tulip entered the kitchen, ubiquitous laptop in hand.

That is weird. "Who's minding the store? And I didn't say anything to Ace. He was in a hurry." I spoke around a mouthful of heavenly cake, using my fork to gesture at her. "And what's the deal with Ivana wanting to bunk with me? Who planted that bright idea in her head?"

Tulip shrugged. "It didn't come from me. If I was going to yank your chain, I'd choose karaoke night. Remember the time Auntie T.J. signed you up to raise money for the new Fire Hall? Ha! You really can't sing, you know, sis."

I gave her the stink-eye. "I am aware."

"Oh, talking about embarrassing moments, don't forget the Bucket Parade on Saturday. Your number's up this time. You should have said no to being a bridesmaid."

"No! Tell me the wedding's *not* this coming Saturday." I slapped my forehead, hoping pain would drive away the image of me climbing into a tractor bucket to be escorted to the nuptials like all the rest of the wedding party.

"Afraid so." Tulip flashed a wicked grin. "Do you need any help? I was just going to close up shop and go home if not. Then I'm heading out to the movie set to see how Star's making out. The whole town must be there by now. Oh, and I promised Granny I'd bring snacks for tonight. She's got Book Club. Got anything available?"

I counted to ten. Very. Slowly. "You didn't think to prepare something, like, I don't know, yourself?"

"Jeez, I'll throw something together now. I just thought since there's so much food already prepared..." She shrugged, giving a cute waggle of her eyebrows, widening her big blue eyes further.

Okay, for Granny. "You can package up an assortment of desserts. That's what they'll all want anyway. Just be a complete waste to take a vegetable tray."

"What time do you want me in the morning?" Suzanna asked, taking off her apron and setting it aside.

"Eight a.m. would be great, if you can manage. We'll need to haul everything over to the location by eleven and start setting up. Can you make it as well, James?"

"Sure. No problemo."

The pair left and I finished tucking the last of the food trays in the cooler then set about making a giant batch of overnight buns to bake in the morning. I sterilized the counters, then surveyed my domain with satisfaction, pleased with having everything in order.

The phone rang, jarring my nerves further. *If one more person needs one more darn thing from me today, I'm not going to be held accountable for the ensuing mayhem.* I stomped over to answer the barking annoyance, picking it up on the seventh ring before it went to the answering machine.

"Tea & Tarot."

"Charm! Thank goodness! Something really awful has happened. Please, you got to get out here. *Now!*" Tulip screamed in my ear.

"What is it? What's wrong?"

"Star...*crackle*..."

"I can't hear you! The line's worse than usual," I complained.

"*Fizz...crackle...*dead!"

"What?" My whole body lurched, the universe stopping spinning. The phone went dead in my hand. *Star? No!*

Chapter Five

Not caring if I got a speeding ticket worthy of an entry in the Guinness World Records book, I thrust Thor's gas pedal into the floorboards with my heaviest leadfoot. We bumped and lurched our way to Spirit Springs, the location of the movie set. It was right on the other side of the lake our town was named after, down a logging road recently graded—I imagined to allow the moving of heavy equipment in for the production company—which meant it was unbelievably dusty from the overturned dirt and gravel. Having left Thor's windows down in my panic, I choked on a mouthful when I slammed on the brakes, narrowly missing a white-tailed buck with impressive antlers who was too busy chasing a female doe fleeing some happy-happy to give me any mind. A hazard for any species.

I parked beside an RCMP SUV, half-falling out of the Jeep in my efforts to locate my sisters. I shielded my eyes with one hand against the glare from the setting sun, scanning the area. A sprawling village of tractors, trailers and equipment that rivaled our town in size greeted me. The steam clouds created by the heat and moisture above the hot springs weren't visible due to the warmth of the day.

Loud noises in the distance alerted me to activity near the springs and I took off at a fast clip down the enlarged path that normally allowed only small terrain vehicles, not dollys and cranes.

"Charm! Over here!"

I stumbled at the sudden edict, turning right around and retracing my steps fifty yards to where my friend Emma stood, furiously windmilling her arms at me.

"What's going on? Who's dead?" I asked, half out of breath and worried sick. It couldn't be anyone close to me, could it? Surely, I would have been getting a premonition if it was?

"It's that accountant guy, Howard something or other."

Thank. You. Goddess. I took a deep breath. "Howard Smith. The guy who's been embezzling funds from the company." I thought back to the negotiations earlier in the day.

"Really? Do you think that had anything to do with his death?" Her green eyes were like saucers in her face surrounded by springy red curls.

Enough about Howard. "What about Star? Is she okay?" I reached out and grabbed hold of Emma. "What happened? Is she all right?"

"She's upset, but she's okay." My pulse slowed down a few hundred beats a second, dropping below hummingbird status.

"Upset by the murder?" I asked, mystified. "Did she find the body?" I couldn't imagine why she'd be upset otherwise — we hardly knew the guy.

"How do you know Howard Smith was murdered?" Constable Ace Collins strode up and stood watching me with an intent expression.

"I don't know for certain, but it was so quick and since he was embezzling—"

"How on earth do you know that?"

"Ah, the usual method." Ace knew all about my ability to read people. He'd even come around to being somewhat supportive during the last murder investigation when it had been proven useful. "We shook hands on a catering deal this morning. Where's my sister and why is she upset?"

Ace looked discomforted. "If you mean Star, she's with Tulip in the nurse's station. Look, she's going to be all right—"

"For heaven's sake! Someone tell me what's going on, or, so help me, I'm going to...to..." I couldn't think of a big enough threat to encompass the frustration of being kept in the dark about family.

"She alleges that Howard Smith, the deceased, attacked her," Ace said.

"*Alleges?* If Star said it happened, it happened. Take me to her. Right. Now." My fury spilled over and my whole body began shaking.

"Of course." Ace took my arm and led me deeper into the camp. Emma trailed along behind us, barely able to keep up the pace. I stomped down the gravel path that led between the trailers and equipment, whipping my head back and forth as I kept a sharp lookout for my sister.

Ace stopped me at a thirty-foot RV clearly marked with medical symbols and a mural of a patient being attending by beaming health personnel in white coats. Similar vehicles drove the highways of Manitoba bringing flu shots, midwifery and medical aid to small prairie towns. "She's in there. But, Charm, there's something you should know—"

I didn't wait but clambered up the steel steps and yanked open the door. "Star! I'm here!"

Tulip popped her head around a curtain at the back, jumped up and half-ran toward me down the narrow aisle of the motor vehicle, her expression not conducive to making me feel any less anxious.

"What's going on?" I asked, grabbing her by the arms and trying to shake the information out of her.

"Star went to see Howard, the accountant, about her paperwork for getting paid, and he made a move on her. Tried to come on to her. She said he was acting really weird, like he was drugged or something. Spooked her. I guess he pushed it even further, grabbing for her. Her necklace came off in the struggle when she pulled away from him and ran from the trailer. She said he was alive when she left him. But, Charm, he was found dead with her pendant clutched in his hand a short time later. It looks so bad. Of course, she had nothing to do with his death, but people are talking." Tulip looked confused as she rambled on. *Probably in shock.*

"I need to see her." I pushed past Tulip and hurried to the back of the RV, thrusting aside the white curtain. Star sat slumped on a reclining chair, a middle-aged woman dressed in powder-blue scrubs attending her. They both looked up, tears filling my sister's eyes when she caught sight of me.

I leaned down and hugged her tight, pressing my forehead against hers. "Are you okay? Did he hurt you?" I whispered. "If you'd gotten yourself killed, I'd never have forgiven you, you little squirt."

"Yeah, I'm okay. He didn't hurt me. I'm just a little shook up." She shuddered.

"And you are?" the woman asked in a professional manner.

"Her sister Charm." I glanced up at her, noting the slight surprise. I got it — we look nothing alike. "I'm the mismatched triplet."

"You're triplets. That's rare," she said. "I'm Violet, by the way."

I nodded. "Nice to meet you. How's my sister doing?"

"She's going to be fine. I just gave her a mild sedative to relax her. A good night's sleep should set her right."

I reached out and grabbed Star's hand. Her ice-cold fingers trembled slightly. I had to see for myself what she had undergone.

"What happened?" I asked. "I need to know. Let me be you — show me." Being triplets, when we chose, we could connect in weird ways. Something I was most grateful for at the moment.

We both closed our eyes and I received a vision of Howard Smith lurching toward me, reaching out with one hand to stop me from leaving his trailer, his eyes dark with lust. Fearful, I stumbled backward and felt a sharp sting on the back of my neck. He got hold of my necklace, tore it from my body. He fell to the floor in a heap, moaning. I fled, tearing down the RV's steps and hitting the ground running, scared out of my wits.

"You didn't touch him," I said when we both opened our eyes.

She shook her head. "No. He was still alive when I hauled butt out of there."

"What are you doing?" Violet asked, frowning.

"Just checking on what happened to my sister. How much later until he was found dead?"

Star slowly shook her head. "Not exactly sure, but not long. I ran into Tulip and she spent a bit of time calming me down, then we heard someone screaming, saying someone was dead — "

"What are you, psychic or something?" Violet interrupted us, her head cocked sideways and her gaze intent.

"A little, maybe." I shrugged it off. "Can I take her home now?"

"There's a Mountie wanting to speak with her." The nurse gave me a look of sympathy.

"Surely you can tell them that it would be better for my sister to wait till morning?"

The sounds of solid footfalls approaching inside the RV did not bode well. Even before I turned around, I knew. *Constable Ace Collins*, large as life, big as a mountain and intense as all get-out, stood staring down at us, his expression stoic.

"I would like to speak with Star alone."

Star's eyes took on that wild-eyed look she got when she was feeling cornered. She silently pleaded with me, mouthing the words, "*Help me.*"

"Constable Collins, I'm taking my sister home now. Arrest me if you want, but I'm not leaving her side."

"Charm — "

Star got up suddenly and pushed past both of us, sending me reeling against a small table covered with implements. It clattered against the wall, its cargo strewn. I lurched into Ace. He reached out and supported me in his strong arms, keeping me from falling to the floor. I glanced at the nurse who appeared stunned, frozen in place.

"Star!" I called out, trying to twist away from Ace in an effort to catch up with my sister. He let me go and I raced down the aisle of the RV, my feet thudding noisily on the floor. I bypassed Tulip and clamored down the steps, Star already ten feet ahead of me. *Oh no!* She wasn't running on the ground away from us — she was literally hovering at least two feet above the ground, as if cushioned by air currents, making her appear to be flying. A small group of people had assembled since we had been inside the nurse's station and they were staring with open mouths, some talking and pointing. *Please, please don't let anyone be capturing this on camera.*

"Star, it's okay! Stop!" I screamed, trying to get her attention before it was too late. She dropped to the ground, her knees bending to absorb the impact, turned and looked toward me. Her horrified expression sent my heart jumping and skittering, trying to run for cover with no place to hide. And there was no place to hide — I caught the glimmer of an iPhone screen, its owner busy filming the moment for posterity.

Chapter Six

I thundered by the animated group, their voices raised in disbelief and their faces aghast at what they had just witnessed. I grabbed hold of Star, hugging her tightly. "It's going to be okay, kiddo, no one's going to harm you. I've got you."

My sister had a terrible fear of confined spaces — a by-product of her first eight years on the planet — and the thought of being hauled off to prison had panicked her. I held on to her until the trembling ceased. I understood. My own phobia rivaled hers. With good reason. We'd both spent hours locked in cupboards.

Footsteps approaching making me spin around. The Mountie was grimacing, looking at me with concern. "She okay?"

"Yeah, no thanks to you. Questioning her like she's guilty? She had nothing to do with this thing! That guy must have had a dozen enemies, embezzling funds like he did. He's even related to that Mafia guy, Guido Morello. Did you know he was married to Morello's cousin?" I forced myself to think. "And what about that poison expert on set? Star said he was acting drugged, pawing at her." I shook my head with disgust at the horrible image. "Maybe that's what killed Howard? He was given a fatal dose of something."

"No, that might have incapacitated him, but it's more than that, Charm. His head was bashed in with blunt force trauma."

My throat went dry, my field of vision narrowing. *To Hades with this.* "When Star left the scene, Howard Smith was alive. I know that absolutely for certain, Ace."

"I still need to take Star in for questioning. She might know something useful."

"Then I'm coming with you."

"Fine."

I took Star's hand in mine, and we walked proudly through the crowd of people who were now pointing and staring at us as if we were a freak show. Yellow police line tape flickered in the breeze, drawing my attention to a trailer roped off with meters of the plastic stuff, *Crime Scene* spelled out in bold black lettering over and over. The image made me angry, furious all over again that my sister had been attacked by that scumbag. Even his death didn't excuse him. Captain Winn Duffy, conversing with another, taller man who appeared to have a human shadow attached in the form of an assistant, drew my attention. The captain stopped in his tracks when he caught sight of us, halting the progress of all three men.

"Constable," he said evenly, giving Star and I a polite nod of greeting. "I'd like you to meet the director of the picture, Dan Carter, and his assistant, Bryce Stanford."

Good. Handshakes forthcoming. I paid close attention while waiting my turn, holding my arm out to shake the director's first. Dan's reading was pretty straightforward. He was concerned for Howard Smith and his family, and worried about how this would affect his production. Bryce ignored the handshaking, not offering his to anyone present. *Germaphobe? Guilty?* I desperately wanted a reading on the guy, but I could hardly jump on his back to take one.

A bystander beckoned at Bryce to get his attention and he moved away. Less than thirty seconds later, he was back, whispering in the director's ear. I watched, frowning as the director's gaze moved over to check out Star, a strange look crossing his face. Bryce thrust a cell phone into the man's hands, sliding his fingers around the screen as if to show him something. I caught the meaning of the interaction, my body tying itself in tight knots. This was bad.

"How the heck—" Dan Carter scratched his scalp under his salt and pepper hair. His mane was slightly on the long side, lying thickly over his red plaid shirt collar. He'd rolled up his shirtsleeves and wore tan trousers with sturdy cowhide work boots, laced up properly. He fit right in. Bryce, on the other hand, was dressed fastidiously, his dark hair recently trimmed to perfection, and wearing a peacock-blue shirt with white buttons accompanied by a darker blue paisley vest. His feet were proudly encased in soft Italian leather oxfords that looked as if they'd cost the GNP of a small country. But the *coup de grâce* was the walking stick he favored. Exquisitely carved. Of course, it might be the most useful thing he had, good for fending off wildlife.

"How is that even possible?" Dan asked, his question accompanied by a bewildered look.

"It's not my fault, any of this!" Star pointed at Ace, then crossed her arms over her chest. "If you hadn't insisted on taking me to the detachment, I never would have made such a dumb mistake. You're the one at fault, Constable."

"Now, it's no one's fault, Star. Constable Collins is just doing his job. That's why we pay him the big bucks," Captain Duffy said in a joking manner. He'd always had the reputation of being the most level-headed man in Snowy Lake. "Show me," he said to the assistant.

He accepted the phone in his big beefy hands and rewound the video with a thumb that half covered the screen, taking a few seconds to preview the footage. Dressed in his RCMP uniform, he made a powerful image, likely choosing to be amiable to make up for how scary he would look if provoked. I'd only heard rumors about the one time he'd lost his temper when a drug dealer had crashed his SUV into the detachment's front foyer after a dangerous chase through town that had ended up causing thousands of dollars' worth of damage to the police building. *Entirely justified.*

It was then I realized that Ace must have seen Star's display when he followed us at such a fast clip out of the nurse's station, and yet had not made a big deal of it. *Classy.*

"My sister was just pulling a Saint Joseph of Cupertino stunt," I joked. *Okay, lame.* Maybe I should have gone with a magician or that nun who loved to fly? A golden oldie Granny Toogood enjoyed on occasion. Of course, Auntie T.J. wouldn't allow herself to be caught dead watching it. Far too tame for our feisty aunt.

"Saint Joseph? Sorry, don't get the reference," Captain Duffy said, his expression puzzled. Now four pairs of eyes studied me like I'd lost my last marble.

"You know, that guy from the seventeenth century. Say, sis, this ability is going to be awesome for dusting hard to reach places and flicking cobwebs from ceiling rafters," I quipped, managing to push myself deeper in the sucking quagmire in trying to stay right away from the harsh reality that *this* was a game changer. A scary game changer.

"Could you keep a lid on this thing for a while? You know, keep the video from going viral?" I asked, desperation causing bile to rise in my throat. I got the distinct impression that two chances existed, slim and none — and slim had left town. But I had to try.

Director Dan frowned. "Sorry, but there's not even the slightest hope of reining this in. It's already been posted. Look." He held out his phone he'd slipped from his pocket, the YouTube video reading five hundred and six views. The numbers changed, clicking ominously upward even while we all peered at the tiny screen. The title under the video read — *Levitating girl tries to outwit Mountie.* Huh, *now* cell phone service improved.

I glanced at Ace. He shook his head, his expression grim.

"Can you do that on demand, Star?" Dan asked, his intense eyes thoughtful.

"Do what?" Star asked, turning her attention to her new boss.

"Levitate like in the video?"

She shrugged. "Maybe. It's kind of a recent development and it's still a bit hit and miss."

"If you would all excuse us, I need to be taking Miss McCall in for questioning," Ace said, his expression pinched, his brown eyes concerned. He was no happier about the situation than I was, but it didn't stop me from objecting. Strenuously.

"No! Star needs to rest. She's exhausted from everything going on," I hissed.

"It's okay, Charm." She put her slender fingers on my arm, giving it a reassuring squeeze. "I can handle this. I've got nothing to hide. Unlike the murderer."

The silence that surrounded us as we continued the walk of annoyance to Ace's vehicle was deafening. I put my arm around Star's slender waist, supporting her if just figuratively. She was handling this better than I'd expected.

Our Queen's own escort opened the back door of the cruiser, standing like a sentinel at the rear of the RCMP vehicle. He waited for us to climb in and closed it behind us. I scooted in beside my sister, catching a whiff of disinfectant unsuccessfully trying to mask the alluring odor of raw skunk.

"What the heck happened in here?" I asked, pinching my nostrils together.

Ace turned the key in the ignition. "Don't ask."

"Aha, I'll bet Tommy and his partner went night hunting again. Right?" Tommy's dog, Slayer, had the uncanny ability to sniff out a skunk within ten miles. *Thinks it's his duty to have his pack leader do something about it. ASAP.* So, Tommy had been sprayed more times then I could remember, ending up in jail when caught red-handed at the activity. Night hunting was illegal for good reason — it was unsafe.

"It's going to be fine, Charm," Star said, bringing my mind reeling back to our present dilemma. Was she trying to reassure me or herself?

"Of course, it is." I squeezed her hand. I was more worried about the video of her levitating than anything else. What to do about the incriminating evidence? I needed to figure a way to squash it before the entire world descended on Snowy Lake, upending our preferred-to-be-left-the-heck-aloneness. *Yes.* An idea popped into my head, bringing a grin to my face. The modern world was going to make this so easy. All I had to do was to add a statement under the video.

No, the Reese's Peanut Butter Cup is not being discontinued. No, Earth will not be plunged into darkness for fifteen days. And NO, Star McCall did not levitate. Ever hear of Photoshop? Or getting some free publicity? Get a life, people.

Star's cell phone gave a long purring sound, reminding me of baby Ling Ling. She answered it after glancing at the number.

"Really? Yes, sure, I can do that!"

She pushed End on the phone, her eyes round and filled with wonder when she gazed over at me.

"What is it?"

"The director just expanded my part. Big time! I'm going to have a major role in the movie, Charm. Can you believe that?"

"Yeah," I sputtered. *No surprise there.* And though it would mean I'd see even less of my sister than usual, I was happy for her. If only a movie would come to town every year, minus any murders, it would work out perfectly. Star would have no need to head to LA. *But the odds of that, not so good.* Unless we began our own production company and I couldn't imagine how many cookies and chocolate slices such a venture would cost. I'd probably have to make enough to ring around the equator a time or two. I loved to bake, but there was a limit.

I gave her a quick hug. "That's great. I imagine he wants to take advantage of your unique talent?"

"Yeah, I guess so. He didn't say that exactly." She frowned. I wasn't sure if the idea of the director wanting her only for her gift bothered her or if the idea of actually having it filmed for posterity was the problem.

"Won't matter. People will just assume it's special effects. Like in the *Superman* movies. And everyone knows how talented you are. They're lucky to have you. Wow, I'm happy for you, sis."

"Thanks."

"Now take me to jail," I quipped at Ace like the character Henry Hill in the Scorsese movie, assuming only I would get the reference.

"Did you really just *Goodfellas* me?" Ace asked, outrage coloring his voice.

"Did you really just use *Goodfellas* as a verb?" I countered, entertained in spite of my concerns about what was happening in our small town — again.

I caught Ace's gaze in the rear-view mirror, his soulful brown eyes about doing me in. My whole body tingled at the connection. Darn it, why did this guy have to have it all? Brains and brawn and to-die-for looks? And yet annoy me to no end with his insistence that I stayed out of things like murder investigations when they affected our town? How was I supposed to do *that* when so much was at stake?

Chapter Seven

Ace jerked the police vehicle into gear, gunned the motor and off we sped. Star glanced at her phone when it purred again. "James says that special item you wanted his brother Alex to make is ready. What special item?"

"Nothing." I said, pleased it was ready so soon considering it had only been a few hours. "A surprise." I grinned at just *how* surprised a certain Mountie was going to be.

The SUV bumped along dusty roads before we hit Main Street. Ace made a right turn at the Clip Joint — the business next to ours — then pulled into the curved driveway in front of the detachment. The low-slung building that housed the RCMP featured a high metal pole out front with our red and white Canadian maple leaf flag proudly flapping in the breeze near the top. It was customary for private citizens to leave bouquets of flowers around the cement base when an officer was killed in the line of duty. When a man died doing his job and trying to protect the rest of us, it broke our collective hearts.

I fumed, waiting for Ace to come around and open the vehicle's door from the outside, the backseat not being a comfortable place to sit. Hard vinyl plastic and not enough leg room were spectacularly unenhanced by the odor of skunk.

I jumped out and Star had to worm her way free. She stood inches taller than me, making her sit with her legs about tucked under her chin. A big man would be scrunched up in a tight ball. Of course, a deliberate design to ensure police protection. It was hard to do much damage squished up in the fetal position.

We marched up the sidewalk and into the station, me holding my sister's hand all the time. No way was the boss man going to separate us without a struggle. Ace picked up on it, apparently, because he motioned for us to follow him into his office. *Good.*

"Have a seat," he said, gesturing at the chairs lined up in front of his desk. I sat, then sighed, checking out the display of flowers and baked goods that threatened to topple off onto the floor. *Again.* The women of Snowy Lake were beyond help, trying to entice the almost-brand-new Mountie. He picked up a few of the items and transferred them to a shelf of a bookcase that sat to one side of his desk. The walls were painted a nice Canadian beige, but a new coat of paint wouldn't have gone amiss. Scuff marks and dints in the dry wall marred the surface in places, making me wonder what tales they could share.

"Okay, down to business." Ace had cleared enough space to open a small black notebook in the center of the mess. He took up a mechanical pencil, then jotted a few things down. He glanced at me first, accompanied by a small smile I think he meant to be reassuring. It was not. *Being in a police station sucks. Big time. Like they can discover all kinds of things you've done in the past.* A prime example was the time I'd ridden double on my friend's bike in grade school and the crossing guard had stopped us, giving us a chewing out for taking a huge safety risk. I'd been certain for days I'd be expelled from school and Granny would be ashamed of me. I couldn't even manage a late library book without anxiety attacks and plying Miriam with stacks of treats, though I thought she deliberately obscured the due date by smearing the fresh ink so I had to jot down on the calendar when I last visited her. *Our librarian does love her sweets.*

"Okay, Star, you said you'd gone to Howard Smith's trailer to fill out some paperwork. Did you do that — fill out the forms?" he asked, his tone well modulated and doing funny things to my insides that I ignored. The walls of the room were closing in on me, ready to squeeze the life out of me. I chewed on my bottom lip, wishing this whole thing was over so I could take my sister home where she belonged. Where I belonged.

"I started to, but he was acting so weird," she said, biting on a glittery pink-colored fingernail. "He got up from his chair, his eyes kind of glazed over and he —" She gave a shudder.

"Is this really necessary?" I demanded, hating that Star had to go through it again. Once was bad enough.

"I'm sorry, but she's the last person known to have seen the deceased alive. Go on, Star, what did he do next?"

"He got up kind of awkwardly, like he was drugged or something, and he lurched toward me, tried to grab hold of me. We struggled — I remember my necklace being torn off — then I somehow managed to pull away. He lost his grip." She shuddered before continuing. "And he fell to the floor, but I could see he was still alive, didn't hit his head or anything."

"We've been over this already! Why don't you find out whose money's in the movie? Oh, and don't forget to check out Guido Morello like I told you. He looks like the kind of guy fully prepared for wet-work."

He didn't look as appreciative as I thought he should be. In fact, he glowered at me. "Did you really just use that term wet-work? I can't believe you even know what it means." He grimaced in distaste. "And yes, Miss McCall, I have all those facts. Thank you very much."

"So why are we wasting time here?"

Star gave me a swift kick to the shins.

"Oww. What was that for?" But at least she looked less upset now.

"Just let the man do his job already."

I took a deep breath. *What would A.C. do?* Agatha Christie always had the answers.

"Did you hear anything else while you were inside the trailer. Any sounds at all?" Ace asked, the expression in his eyes pinning me in place before he turned his full attention to Star.

"You think the murderer was already inside when my sister was there?" My pulse instantly hit its highest setting, my mouth dry.

"It's possible." Ace raised one eyebrow. "His body was discovered a short time later. Problem is, no one else was seen leaving his trailer after Star."

"Who discovered the body?"

Ace hesitated for a split second, then decided to share, probably knowing I could sleuth it out in record time.

It wasn't as though anyone else could do what I could to get to the truth, Mr. Fancy-smancy Master's Degree in Criminology aside. Okay, I'd give him that—it was something all right. *But book learning's not real-life knowledge, no way, no how.*

"Felicity Higgins, the daughter of the woman in the starring role, Mimi Blake, and one of the makeup persons, Sharon Jennings. They wanted to see Howard about an accounting matter to do with a discrepancy in Sharon's paycheck."

"The poison expert? Now *there's* a prime suspect for you."

Ace pursed his lips, clicking the point of his pencil against the tabletop.

"Looks like you've got two suspects already. And I didn't like the look of that PA. What was his name? Yeah, Bryce Stanford. Never trust a man who won't shake hands, my granny always says. And there was another guy that had a beef with Howard. Some guy called Chace. And check out that money trail like I mentioned. Now, can I take my sister home?"

The pencil lead snapped off the mechanical implement before it flew across the desk, landing in my lap. "Chace Wilde—that's the guy you met in the café?" he asked.

"A very good friend of Howard's, if you get my drift. Need a sharpener, Sheriff?" I hid my grin, picking up the sliver of lead delicately between thumb and forefinger and depositing it in the white plastic-lined garbage can beside his desk. Why did I enjoy winding up the man so much? I had no idea, but it was a lot of fun. Could it perhaps be some payback for his insistence that I stayed out of things that deeply concerned me? *Nah, I'm not that incorrigible. I'll leave that to my sisters.*

"Yes, you may go. But don't leave town. And as for you, Charm, stay the heck out of things or I promise you will not like where they lead," he growled, his tone vibrating through my bones and making me fantasize about jumping across the desk and kissing him on his fine lips, sister watching the show or not.

"Aye aye, Captain." I saluted him with one hand to my forehead, quite unclear of the wisdom of baiting him further. It just felt darn good. *Cut me a little slack. Who doesn't feel a little crazy in police stations?*

"I mean it, Miss McCall. If you interfere with this police investigation, I will throw you in jail so fast that your head will spin faster than that girl's in *The Exorcist*. Consider yourself warned."

"Fine," I said, my lips twitching from holding back.

"Expect to see me later." He looked good sitting at his desk, his handsome face pinched by chagrin, and clutching the mechanical pencil.

I gave him a stiff nod and grabbed Star's hand again. I took off with her in tow, barreling down the corridor between the offices at a fast clip, then pushing open the front door of the detachment.

"Hey! Slow down," Star protested.

"I've got food to finish preparing and a kitchen to clean. You going to help?"

"Jeez, what's the big deal? You shouldn't let the constable get to you like that. He was just investigating what happened between me and Howard Smith."

I turned and looked at her when we made the street. A sudden pang of guilt for what she had just been through sent me into a tailspin.

"I'm sorry, Star, I shouldn't have taken it out on you. He just pushes my buttons when he doesn't realize how much help I can be. I mean, who else can get a reading on suspects?"

She patted my arm. "Oh, I think he thinks you're *a lot* of help."

I narrowed my eyes at her. Was my sister dissing me now?

"Yes, I can be," I said, blowing at a strand of hair that had fallen across my forehead. I stopped walking at the door to the Tea & Tarot and turned to Star. "And I intend to be a lot more help."

She shook her head. "You didn't hear a word he said, did you, sis?"

"Blah, blah, blah. But you wait and see, tomorrow when we deliver the food to the set, I've got the time to do some investigating of my own. Easy-peasy."

"I don't know that you should be sticking—"

"Star! This affects our family."

"Yeah, but since I didn't do it, why—"

"The quicker this is all cleared up, the better for everyone. Just leave it to me. I got a very special skill set just waiting to be unleashed on the murder suspects."

Star shook her head. "I don't think the constable really wants your help. And I got the feeling he believes I'm innocent anyway and will find the real killer."

What's the fun in that? For all his threats during the last murder investigation, I'd escaped unscathed. Okay, he had thrown me in jail that one time, but my coven sisters had gotten me right out again by protesting and burning an effigy of our sweet Mountie on the front lawn of the detachment. *Note to self—Explain to the crew not to make a habit of that kind of thing, even if it works.*

"I didn't read all those books on how to solve crimes and understand a murderer's mind to just sit on the sidelines. Let me handle this. I gotcha covered."

"Okay, but don't say I didn't warn you. You know what happened last time."

"And I solved the crime, with a little help, eh."

I patted her on the back and opened the café door, ushering her inside. No one was around, which meant the two of us could spend some quality time together. "Up for some time in the kitchen?" *Best mood changer for me is cooking for others.* "I still need to do a Kismet Spell to bless all the food before we deliver it tomorrow. Want in?"

"I would, but I'm a bit tired. I wouldn't add any power to it. And I've got an early call tomorrow. The director wants me on set at first light to discuss my new role. Isn't that something? This is going to be my big break — I can feel it in my bones, Charm. You know, the cards said this would happen soon. They've been speaking of good things to come for days now."

"Okay, but make sure you're never alone with a male again. Promise me."

She gave a huge put-upon sigh. "I don't want to be seen as difficult to work with."

"Better difficult than in difficulties." I shook my head with misgivings. "You're so young and vulnerable."

"That's rare! We're exactly the same age and yet you run all over town doing whatever you darn well please."

"Not exactly the same age."

"I gotta go before I say something I'll regret. Bye." She turned abruptly and stomped from the café, probably on her way to sleep at Granny Toogood's. It was still the family home. I had lucked out and lived in the apartment above the café. *Oh goddess, that reminds me.* I needed to discuss living arrangements with our Ivana, before I was left without a place to sleep. No way was I laying my head down alongside the sister of a Russian Bratva. *I just might lose it.*

Ling Ling strolled up, circling my jean-clad legs with her purr engine set at maximum overdrive while leaving a fluffy trail of evidence. I didn't worry about the fur settling on the treats laid out in vast profusion over the counters — the trays were covered with plastic lids.

"We thank you for this bounty of the sacred Earth. May this food be safe and nourishing to all who consume it and bless them with optimal health, gifting them energy, vigor and well-being." I sent my positive intentions out into the universe, visualizing the stream as a circle of love, enjoying the tug on my spirit and the answering karma of sunlight entering the deepest parts of my soul.

"Good stuff, eh, Ling Ling? You hungry?"

She tilted her head to the side, giving me the look she was famous for and that was best summed up in one word — *Duh.*

"Hmm, smoked salmon pâté or chicken liver? One meow for salmon, two for liver."

"*Meow, meow, meow.*"

"Ah, wise choice. A bit of both."

Ling Ling watched my actions critically as I spooned out a few treats onto a china plate, lining them up in a perfect checkerboard pattern. I laid the plate on a mat and set it in front of her. She took a few polite nibbles of the pâté, then delicately licked her paws.

"You're lucky you're a cat, you know. There's this new interloper in town after the new Mountie."

She cocked her head at me, her deep blue eyes a brilliant contrast to the whiteness of her fur.

"I knew you'd understand. She's a real gold-digger, too. A geologist by trade." I snorted.

Ling Ling gave a bit of a snuffle and a couple of disgusted sneezes, obviously in utmost sympathy for my plight.

"I know, I know. But what's a gal to do? I can't just go and drag my prey in like you could. Besides, if he doesn't come freely, then what's the point? I want my romance — when the goddess deems it time — to be of the big variety. You know, to have my Prince Charming sweep me right off my feet. Call me old-fashioned, but I want to be shown without a shadow of a doubt that I'm the right woman for him, and he's the right man for me."

A throat cleared behind me, making the hairs on the back of my neck prickle. I whirled around, the subject of our debate looming over me. "What are you doing sneaking up on me?" What the heck, was he psychic? He seemed to have an uncanny ability to show up at *exactly* the wrong moment.

Chapter Eight

"Who are you talking to? You didn't hear me knocking because you were so deeply engrossed in conversation, Miss McCall. What would you have done if I was a bad guy? Keep your doors locked, please. There's another murderer afoot," Constable Ace Collins said, his expression tight.

Ling Ling gave another scoffing sneeze. She prided herself on her spectacular hearing, and she was right, she could hear a mouse fart at fifty paces. And with that she rolled her eyes and exited stage right, tail swishing.

"So, you just let yourself in? And what's your definition of a 'bad guy' anyway? Does it include someone who sneaks up and scares a person?" I crossed my arms over my chest, mortified to be caught talking with a feline about my nonexistent love affair. "And I was discussing philosophy with Ling Ling. She's studying Stoicism." *There, make of that what you will.*

His eyes bugged out a little bit. *Ha!*

"You know, you don't need to make up stories to get my attention. I just came by to touch base and bring you this." He held out the book he'd mentioned earlier. "Not a grand gesture on a scale of one to ten, but a mark of respect for your brilliant mind, Miss McCall."

"Ahh, thanks." I accepted the book, ignoring his poke about a grand gesture and glanced at the cover. *Real Magic.*

"Who was that guy I saw you with earlier?" he asked, casual-like.

"Who? Oh, you mean James, the guy I just hired to be my new helper? Why, what about him?" *Yikes.* Had he heard what I was up to with his brother?

He didn't answer but moved a step closer, his expression shifting. Was it my imagination or was he looking a tad smugger than he had been just a second ago? I set the book down on the counter and looked up, way up. He leaned in toward me, using the back of his hand to caress my cheek with gentle swipes of his knuckles, garnering my full attention. "And we have other unfinished business, if I'm not mistaken. Something promised earlier. You have such beautiful skin," he murmured.

Oh, but he's *beautiful.* Chocolate brown eyes with long dark, curling lashes. Tan skin, his square jaw sporting a five o'clock shadow. He was still wearing his uniform and the officialness of it stirred me, adding another layer of danger between us.

The world hushed. He slipped an arm around me and tugged me to him. I breathed in his woodsy masculine scent, my body beginning to vibrate at a whole different frequency. Then it happened. He captured my lips with his.

The first touch of his warm mouth sent an electrical charge coursing through me. The heat of his body radiated into mine, the combination instantly deadly. Each nerve, each cell, each fiber of my being came alive. A wash of sensation pulled me away from the real world and made this moment — this incredible moment — matter far too much. Something was awakening within me. Something wild and free. His kiss — I couldn't understand or escape it.

A vision arose in my mind. Me, making a pact with the man branding me with each thrust of his tongue, each slide of his lips over mine. Him, getting me to promise him something. *I don't care what it is, just keep kissing me...*

He broke the kiss and ran a fingertip over my swollen lips. "You are an amazing kisser, darlin'."

I couldn't speak. Too many sensations swirled inside me. Surely a kiss shouldn't cause me to lose it?

"Cat got your tongue?" he teased, adding with a full-on grin, "Didn't seem to earlier."

I cleared my throat, the ground still shifting under my feet. "What do you think you're doing, sending me a vision of me kowtowing to your demands? Planting ideas? Right! Like I'd ever agree. That's low."

"It was worth a try, darlin'," he said, not looking one tiny bit sorry. In fact, even smugger.

"Just so you know, it won't work. You know I can help you. You testing me, Ace?"

"How about we work a deal, darlin'?" His warm body remained so close to mine, making me want another kiss. Would kiss number three be just as good? I wanted to do some testing of my own...

"Maybe. What are the terms?" I hedged.

"I call you when I want you to check someone out. Otherwise, you stay out of things. I can focus better, do my job better, if I know you're safe."

"Hmm," I stalled. I had plans for tomorrow, plans that included checking out an idea that had come to me earlier tonight. I couldn't afford to have my hands tied, even by this big, tall, strapping Mountie. Now what would that be like? The idea held some merit…

"You think about it. We could make a good team doing things the official way. I should be going now," he said. Disappointment filled me that he had given up so easily. Surely another bribe was in order?

"Ah, yeah, I need to get to bed, too." *Bed.* Why mention that place? A part of me wanted to drag him by the hand up the staircase and see just where that would lead, while another part, a far smarter part, was horrified. *And what if you lose your goddess-given gifts, sweeting?* Granny Toogood's voice filled my mind, settling the matter. Nothing like thinking of my granny to cool the ardor. Besides, there had been no definite sign that he was 'The One'. But what did I expect to happen? Some otherworldly voice intervening and giving the go-ahead? *Life is never that easy or clear-cut.* I had to take this in little tiny baby steps, even though my body was giving the green light to head right on past third base and slide into home plate. I licked my lips. Baseball had never sounded so sexy or hot to me before.

He stepped back and a space opened between us, helping to halt the insanity.

"Sleep well, darlin'."

"You know I will," I said, adding a grin to make sure he would be uncertain of how much his mere physical presence influenced me. Thank goodness he couldn't read visions. He'd be encouraged all the more and we'd be upstairs in a flash. That was, if I still had an upstairs available with Ivana working so hard to give it away.

"Oh, that reminds me, my parents are coming for a visit this weekend. If you're free Saturday night, I'd like you to join us for dinner."

"Who else will be there?" I asked, though disappointment filled me that I had a wedding to attend I couldn't dare skip. Not unless I wanted to be skinned alive by Melody and Mick, the bride and groom, not to mention the wedding party consisting of a slew of Northern Lights Coven members. Thank goodness the stag and shower had been last week, or that would tie up another night.

I glanced at Ace when he didn't respond right away. Was that a blush? So, She Who Would Not Be Named would be there. Now I was plenty annoyed that I couldn't attend.

"Jennifer Morgan's an old family friend. If you'd give her a chance, I think you'd like her."

I pasted an innocent look on my face. "What makes you think I don't like her? I've been nothing but nice to her, even offering free treats. But I'm sorry, I'll have to take a rain check. I have a wedding to attend on Saturday night." Was that a hint of disappointment reflected in his eyes?

He shrugged. "She thinks you might misconstrue things. You know, think that our going back so far makes you uncomfortable. She wanted me to say that she'd like for the two of you to become friends."

"Take it from me, nothing she could say or do would affect anything I already know about her. And I already have more friends than I can keep up with. But I do wish her well."

He frowned, as if trying to decipher my words but not finding anything wrong with them. *Good.* I had Jennifer's number. *Six, six, six.*

"As you wish…"

"Did you just *Princess Bride* me?" I held back the laughter. Okay, fair recompense for the *Goodfellas* quote.

"Did you just use *Princess Bride* as a verb?" A grin flashed on his handsome mug. *Oh my.* When he was filled with such glee, he looked ten years younger, the stern Mountie façade melting clear away. The image tugged at me.

"Good night, Ace."

"Good night, darlin'."

I watched him saunter from the kitchen, knowing the spring in his step was my doing.

I glanced around the kitchen. What was left to do? Nothing that couldn't wait till morning. And so, to bed. I climbed the stairs with a light step, looking forward to time alone to savor the recent conversation. *Please, please, let Ivana be asleep.* I slowed down, creeping on tiptoe by her door, not wanting another altercation.

Her suite door flew wide open. "Ah, Charm. We talk."

"Could this wait? I'm exhausted."

She crossed her arms over her spectacular breasts, a pout beginning on her full lips with their perfect coating of *femme fatale* lipstick. "No time for best friend?"

I pasted a bright smile on my face. *Best to get it over with.* "Sure. I have a couple of minutes. Then I must get to bed, I have an early morning."

"I got boarder to bring in money for friend."

I held back a groan. "Really? When and who?" No point in asking the why. Ivana always did what she wanted.

"Lady. Makes wolf faces." She wrinkled her nose at the idea.

A lightbulb moment. "Right. The special effects person who applies silicone appliances and makeup and dresses people to look like wolves."

"What I say." Ivana was all indignant that I'd just repeated her information in a coherent manner.

"Yes, of course. When is she scheduled to start staying with us?" *Please, not tonight.*

She made a face. "Not today. Foolish."

I tried not to look too relieved. "Yes, very. Tomorrow?"

"Yes. She come tomorrow."

"And what shall I call this person? Does she have a name?"

Ivana narrowed her eyes, giving me a glimpse of her former life in Russia. "Miss Regina is title. She hates murder. We should ask others to come. Live here. Be safe."

"No! Please, there's no room!" I was so horrified I forgot myself for a second. I could only envision rows and rows of cots and bunks set up in every available nook and cranny. I leaned against her doorframe to keep myself upright, my knees refusing to function.

"Money." She rubbed her thumb and forefinger together in the universal gesture.

"No more money necessary." I shook my head so firmly I gave myself an instant concussion. "I'm going to make lots doing the new catering job for the movie set."

"Yes?" Her expression changed again. "No more money? Ah, maybe I not pay now? Get—what you say in Canada—commission?"

"Yes, fine. You don't have to pay if, and only if, *you don't invite anyone else to stay here.* You understand? In fact, you cancel Miss Regina's contract for my suite, and I'll pay you, say, fifty dollars a month on top of your free room and board." *Certifiable. That's me.* But when negotiating with Ivana I was more than used to getting the Russian end of the stick.

"Nice." A huge smile lit up her gorgeous face. "I take care of her."

Some feeling came back into my legs as a little of the stress drained and I pushed away from her doorjamb. *Wait.* On second thoughts, I'd better clarify or the movie might be minus one special effects person. "Ah, you will be kind when you explain things to Miss Regina? Let her down gently?"

She pounded her hand into her chest in the general location of her heart. "Ivana make Charm promise. Miss Regina gone."

"I don't *literally* want her gone."

She shook her head, obviously not getting my meaning.

"Not *gone*, okay?"

"Not gone?" Now she looked confused.

"Still at movie set. I want her to be able to keep working. Just not living with us, but *living*. Alive, not dead. You understand?"

"Hmm. Okay. Ivana gets it."

Jeez. Just in case, I'd better send out a protection spell to help the unsuspecting woman. "Good night, Ivana."

"Good night, my friend." She tugged me to her and double-kissed both cheeks. I was so relieved that we'd straightened things out that I did the same back with extra enthusiasm.

Like we were about to be separated for years and years, she gave me a lengthy farewell in the form of long ongoing hand waves and multiple air kisses until I'd shut my apartment door behind me. I took a deep breath and tugged off my shoes. I walked straight to the bedroom and face-planted on my bed, too exhausted to bother doing one more thing. Of course, things never worked out as planned.

Chapter Nine

Morning came too early. I'd spent most of the night tossing and turning, worried about Granny and how the doctor had insisted she take time off from working at the café and put up her feet with their swollen ankles. Then I'd stewed about the exasperating Mountie situation. What *exactly* was going on between us? I crawled off my bed at first light, wishing I could ask our librarian Miriam for a useful book on male–female relationships that didn't make me roll my eyes in exasperation. Really, was all that compromise so often suggested by the authors who wrote those books going to help a situation where a person *had to* find their true mate? *Not freakin' likely*.

I stumbled into the bathroom and hit the shower. Three cups of scalding-hot black coffee and I was back to functioning. I took the stairs down to the kitchen two at a time, my caffeine buzz propelling me into fast-forward mode.

I had the second batch of the special cloverleaf buns already baking when James and Suzanna arrived at eight.

"Mornin', guys."

James gave a low whistle, checking out the counters. "Did you leave anything for us to do?"

I laughed, still high on the dark brew. "Don't worry, lots of chores to go around. I wonder what the deal is on set? Do we need to bring our own portable tables?"

"I'll check for you," James said. He pulled a wrapped item out of his backpack. "And look, here you go. Alex says no charge if you'll send me home with some of your famous death-by-chocolate slice."

"Thanks." I took the package from him, unwrapped it and ran my forefinger lovingly over the engraving. Slipping it in my pocket, I gave James a huge grin. "Tell him it looks good."

"What do you want me to do first?" Suzanna asked, washing her hands then tying on an apron.

"Add the diced chicken to the Caesar salad trays, please, then start packaging up the buns. They can go into my Jeep first. Can we use your car as transport? Otherwise it's going to be a few trips."

"Sure."

I decided then and there that Suzanna was goddess sent.

By ten-thirty, everything was set. Between the three vehicles — James also got the loan of his parents' SUV — we'd managed to pack everything in. Convoy-style, we hit the road. Fortunately, we didn't have to bring our own tables, or we'd have been tying those to the roof as well.

Bumping along the road, trying to keep the speed low without stalling Thor's motor or raising a humungous cloud of dust, I went over everything we still needed to do. *The first time is the hardest,* I reassured myself, hoping tomorrow I'd be able to leave my antsy nerves at home. I packed close to the staging area for lunch to avoid lugging the trays of food any farther than necessary, then opened the back door of my Jeep.

"Well, well, if it isn't our pretty little caterer." The man attached to the smarmy tone confronted me, fingers locked in his belt loops. Guido Morello.

"I'm sorry about your brother-in-law," I said, maneuvering a tray of food out of Thor and hefting it against my hip to support it for the short journey to the catering tent.

"Yeah, thanks." He didn't look that upset. *Hmm.* "Need my help?" he asked.

"I'm fine, thanks. My crew's on it."

"Anything you need, you don't hesitate to ask. Guido's always ready to be of service to such a pretty lady."

"Good to know," I said briskly, edging my way around him. "Do you mind?" His kind of 'service' was as helpful as a huge boulder blocking the path.

"Of course," he said, moving a few millimeters to one side. I sighed and proceeded to brush past him. His overpowering cologne made my nose seize up, the fresh country air disappearing in an instant, replaced with a stuffiness I knew from long experience would last for hours.

He followed me, my self-appointed bodyguard, all the way to the catering tent, chatting me up. Guido was surprisingly easy to hear over the humming diesel generators housed in tractor-trailers lined up nearby, providing the camp with electricity. Had the camp managers also thought to hire Henry's Honeywagon to empty the RV tanks? It would be a good contract, considering the amount of BS I was being subject to this morning, pun intended.

"A gal who looks like you can't be too careful about who she hangs around with. You know what I'm sayin', sweetheart? I'm a-gonna take a special interest in making sure you stay safe. That's a promise. And Guido Morello never breaks a promise. There's a murderer on the loose, you know?"

"Yes. I heard. But I think I'm perfectly fine in broad daylight. Don't let me take up your time, Mr. Morello. You must have a lot on your plate."

"Please, call me Guido. No need to stand on conventions here. On set, we're just one big happy family." Heavy footsteps crunching on gravel approached, drawing both our attention. *Yes*. Any interruption would be appreciated. Even the Grinch who stole Christmas would have gotten a handwritten thank-you note about then.

"Morning, Miss McCall." Constable Ace Collins tipped his hat at me. "Guido." *So, no fonder of Gangster Guy than me.*

"Morning, Sheriff," I said, adding a cheeky grin over my nasally greeting, my nose still plugged. He repaid me with a twinkle of his brown eyes.

"It's Constable, as you're well aware. You're sounding a bit stuffed up this morning, Miss McCall. You coming down with something?" he asked.

"I'm allergic to toxic levels of perfume, cologne and pollen, among other things," I said, slanting my eyes with discretion toward the interloper and adding a slight grimace.

"Mr. Morello, if I may have a few minutes of your time," Ace said. The polite wording was not phrased as a question.

"Sure, Sir." A wolfish grin accompanied the man's acceptance. *Like he has a choice in the matter.* Constable Ace Collins obviously followed the Mounties' creed of 'always get your man'. The RCMP had undertaken the obligation in the days of Sam Steele and the beginnings of the North West Mounted Police long before having been renamed the Royal Mounted Canadian Police. Hmm. Then why did I feel such a need to assist our almost-new Mountie? *A question for another time.*

"I'll be back later, pretty lady. Don't go anywhere, ya hear?" Guido loosed his parting shot, making the fine hairs on the back of my neck stand up.

It was Ace's turn to grimace, the expression in his brown eyes changing to solid ice. *Interesting.*

The pair moved off, the big tall Mountie striding with all proper decorum and stiffness while the far shorter Boston gangster rolled along as if he was practicing to board a pirate ship. I went back to my job of setting up and sent a prayer to the universe that I would be able to find the opportunity I needed most today, a chance to slip into Howard's trailer unseen.

My two helpers joined me and, before the appointed hour, a swarm of locusts of biblical proportions – aka the movie people and actors – descended on our enclave, cleaning us out of every scrap of food in no time flat. Shocking. And apparently it was first come, first served, with everyone reaching over and around each other, jostling – mostly amiably – while grabbing the greatest amount of food they could before scurrying away. Some even stuffed their pockets and others had brought their own plastic containers or shopping bags. What had I signed us up for?

"Has no one ever fed these people before?" I grumbled to no one in particular. Even my own sister had done a grab and run, promising to catch up later.

"That was weird, all right," Suzanna said with a frown, busy piling up empty containers that barely needed washing, they'd been picked so clean.

"Well, I hope there was enough food? We brought plenty for a hundred and fifty people, for heaven's sake." I frowned at the forlorn carrot stick left on one tray, the only morsel in sight, expecting a mouse to hop up, nab it in its tiny paws and tear off with it.

"I think they're trying to get two meals out of one. You know, save having to worry about supper later. I overheard some people talking about that being the plan," James said.

"Well, I hope everyone's eaten. There's nothing left." Hours and hours to prepare, and sixty seconds to vanish. *Some feat.* This set was working magic in more ways than just the title and having my sister onboard. Well, it did leave time for a bit of sleuthing around before I got down to preparing another feast for the world's hungriest crew.

"Okay, can you handle getting the trays back to the café? I want to look around a bit."

"Sure, we'll start on tomorrow's lunch and help man the café," Suzanna said. "Take all the time you need. We got this. Oh, by the way, my sister Nancy said she could come by and help, if you needed her?"

"Great idea." That would free me to spend time on solving the case. We were stretched a tad thin at the moment between the catering contract and the café. "I think we'd better consider making ten percent more of everything for tomorrow." I sighed. That would eat into profits, but I couldn't live with myself if even one person went hungry.

I carried a load of trays to Suzanna's cherry-red Mazda and piled them in the trunk. "Okay, that does it. I'll be back soon."

"No rush. We got this."

"Thanks."

Giving the pair a quick wave, I headed back into camp. *Woman on a mission.* Or was that PI? *Nah, honorary RCMP officer better fit the bill.* Now, if I could just get Ace to agree, we'd be all set. I stopped about twenty feet from Howard's trailer. The police tape was still in evidence, the home on wheels forlorn and deserted-looking. *Yes, please, stay like that.* I reconnoitred the area, striding around my target until I had circled it. Twice. Two doors, situated one at each end of the thirty-foot RV. So, the murderer hadn't exited that way or someone would have seen them. *Time to test my theory.*

I gave a look around—no one in sight. It was now or never. I crept up the short staircase, trying not to make any noise on the steel rungs. Soft-soled running shoes helped. Twisting the handle, I pulled the door open and slipped inside the darkened space, to shut the door quickly behind me. I let out a deep breath. So far, so good.

I remained still for a few seconds, listening to the ambience and breathing in an odor that was less than pleasing. The floor and walls must still hold evidence of the killing. To my right was the hallway that likely led to the bedrooms and bathroom. I gave a courtesy check of the room that had been used as Howard's office, not expecting to find anything in the communal section. Seeing the blood pooled on the linoleum turned my stomach, and I kept my gaze averted, gingerly stepping around the splatter. Howard must have been hit pretty hard to bleed out like that. Satisfied that there was no more to be learned, I crept down the hallway and slid the first door on its track. To save room, all the doors were of the sliding variety. They vanished into the walls when opened.

Stepping inside the tight confines of the bathroom, I surveyed the space, using my hands to check for crannies and to knock against the walls. Nothing. I moved on to the next room, a bedroom, and gave it a thorough going over. I hurried into the final room — another bedroom. This had better be it or my theory didn't hold water.

A built-in clothes cupboard held promise. I slid the shirts and pants on plastic hangers to one side, trying but failing to ignore the fact that a man had been alive and wearing these very items just yesterday. The scent of floral fabric softener stirred up by my snooping made the experience a bit easier. Hmm, my nose must have been unplugging from the stench of Guido's cologne if I could detect lilacs and pine.

I checked at the base of the closet and found a wooden section under a pile of clothes. I bundled the clothes aside and gave the area a quick knock. Hollow. *Yes.* Was this it?

Was someone at the door? *Crap.* Using my nonexistent fingernails and cringing at the sudden pain in my fingertips, I pried up the wide planks that were locked together, creating a two foot by three foot opening that led down under the trailer. *A well-hidden trap door without a convenient hook to hold it open.* Setting the piece of lumber upright against the back of the closet — fortunately it was hinged at the base — I climbed inside, then jumped down to the ground under the mobile home. Pleased with my awesome discovery, I stayed crouched, peering at the earth underneath, checking for shoe marks or other evidence. Nothing. It appeared swept clean.

I glanced back up through the open section one last time. And right into the stern face of Constable Collins. *Oh, fudge.*

"Hey, Ace, look what I found!" I said brightly, then rolled away and out of sight. I jumped to my feet once I was free of the trailer's edge. *Time to go.* I'd done my duty, pointed out how the murderer had gotten away. *Easy-peasy.*

I took the last corner at an even faster pace, my target in sight. Thor. Just a few more steps and I'd be on my way. *Halleluiah.*

"Miss McCall! Halt! Stop right where you are!"

Could I pretend I hadn't heard him? Probably not. I'd lost my momentum anyway. I leaned against Thor, arms crossed over my chest, waiting for the Mountie to catch up.

"What is it, Sheriff?" I asked. "I'm in a bit of a rush—"

Ace pressed his lips together. *Uh-oh.* My pulse lurched at how dark and angry his eyes had turned. Time to lighten this mood. And I had just the thing.

I reached into my pocket and pulled out the shield. "In case you're wondering, I do have clearance to be here."

Brows knitted together, he looked down at my outstretched hand. I held Alex's recent handiwork out to him on my palm, waiting for him to inspect it. My special offering.

"What the—"

"And if you look carefully, you'll see I'm a pay grade above you." He reached out and nabbed it before I could thrust it back in my pocket for safekeeping. After all, it was costing me more than a few death-by-chocolate slices.

"Miss McCall, are you aware that impersonating an RCMP officer is a federal offense?"

"Duh, if you look closely, it says 'honorary'. You know, they do that with university degrees all the time. In fact, you gave me the idea, so if you're going to blame anyone, blame yourself. And if I remember correctly, you said these very words to me yesterday — *if I ever catch you interfering with an official investigation ever again without your name stamped on a police shield...* So, I fixed it. Got my own official police identification gear. Of course, I had to make a trade for it. But fair's fair. So, you can rest assured that my hiney is covered, Sheriff."

He shook his head, chewing on his bottom lip as he studied the shield, then looked at me. How was this going to play out? Best guess, he'd argue that I had misunderstood his intention. But then the sweetest thing happened. He broke out laughing. A marvelous sound, a warm chuckle. It bubbled up from deep inside his broad chest, spilling out into the air filled with waves of pure merriment. Heartwarming. And suddenly all was right with the world. His brown eyes turned to chocolate cream as he laughed, enticing and exciting all at the same time. *Charisma.* He had it in spades. Oh my...

I think I fell a bit in love with him, right then and there.

Chapter Ten

"Okay, Miss McCall, you win. I will forgive this indiscretion, just this once. But you are aware you were disturbing a crime scene?"

"I was careful. I didn't step in the blood or anything. I just needed to know how the real murderer escaped, you know? To defend and protect my sister?" I was reeling from my recent thoughts on how I felt about this gorgeous man. How had that happened? What could I be thinking using the *L* word so soon, even if just to myself? I'd only known Ace a few weeks. But I admired him so much when he wasn't busting my chops over something that I had no choice but to do that it must have crept up on me. Or maybe it was just relief at having escaped another lecture. *Better to think that.* I set the whole Big *L* idea aside and gave him my full attention.

"So, I'm free to leave?"

"Of course, but I will be keeping this for the time being." He put my shiny new RCMP badge in the shirt pocket of his uniform and gave me a direct look, clearly stating, *I'll be keeping an eye on you, darlin'*.

Fine. Do that. I'm countin' on it, big man.

I opened Thor's driver's-side door and slid onto the seat that was warm from the morning sun pouring in his windshield. I was about to insert the key in the ignition when a sudden knock on the glass startled me. *Ace.* I rolled down the window.

"Yes?" His fragrance of leather and soap drifted in. I took a deep breath. *Lovely.*

"Before you go, I'd like your reading on someone. If you have the time?"

Do I! "Sure. I can always find the time for you." Oops, better rein the enthusiasm in or I'd have some explaining to do.

"Great. I'd appreciate it, darlin'." He smiled, then moved back, politely opening the driver's door so I could disembark. My heart grew about three sizes at that precise moment. *Enjoy. Because you know nothing ever stays the same, sweeting. My granny's exact words.*

"They're out at the springs," he said, directing me to come with.

I pretty much bounced on the balls of my feet all the way down the widened path toward Spirit Springs, content to be at his side and not fighting him for a change. The air seemed sweeter, the clouds fluffier, the grass greener. *Maybe there's something to this working together, eh, Constable?* Because he looked happy too. The only thing that would have added to the experience was if we held hands and were on our way to a picnic…

The road ended at a clearing.

We stopped in tandem, staying just inside the tree line to observe the action. The entire area was lit by an enormous lamp pouring its light onto the actors' faces. Dan Carter, the movie's silver-maned director I'd met yesterday, stood like a Siamese twin with the camera operator to catch all the action, his posture tense.

"Okay, everyone, clear the sight line, please," the tall man shouted over the fray. All human-made sound died, allowing the rustling of some small creatures in the bush to be heard.

"Scene Four — Take One." A loud slap of a hinged stick onto a diagonal striped slate by the clapper boy followed.

"Action!"

I stood fascinated, and a bit nervous. Even though it was the twenty-first century, the scene unfolding before me was right out of Dante's *Inferno*.

In the center of the clearing a beautiful woman was tied to a stake, her long red hair flowing down to her hips and rushes piled around her feet. A crowd, their faces alight with a rabid, almost inhuman lust, circled, taunting and shouting at the woman.

"Burn the witch! Burn her and send her straight to hellfire!"

"Ye shall not suffer a witch to live!"

Missiles of rotten foodstuff flew, punctuating their damning words, drenching the woman's bodice with disgusting decay. She was a marvel, only straightening her spine and staring out at the unwashed ignorant — aka quaintly dressed period extras — as though they were dirt beneath her dainty feet.

A mountain of a handsome-hero type came striding forward with obvious purpose through the crowd. The two main actors stared at each other across the open meadow while the dark-hooded executioner with his burning stick knelt before the priest, asking formal forgiveness for his actions. Then he hurried to light the faggots of dry timber surrounding the stake. Wind machines were turned on and the fire danced like a hungry beast, well away from the heroine though on film it would appear much nearer. Several firemen huddled nearby, awaiting instruction, in the event that anything went wrong with the stunt.

"Goddess forgive them, for they know not what they do," the witch spoke out with true conviction, but it only made the crowd redouble its efforts, throwing more foodstuffs and screaming profanities.

The hero moved more quickly now, pushing aside the cowards and hurrying to untie her bound hands. He bore her up in his strong arms and raced back into the woods with her, vanishing behind a cloak of green. A bit cliché, but not bad either. It stirred my imagination, a white knight rising up and bearing me away to his private lair. I shivered, my mind and body unsettled by the vision.

"Print," Tom Dawson shouted over the roar of the wind machines, ending the magic. The fireman hurried forward to extinguish the few flames of fire remaining after the fuel was switched off. "Thank you all for getting it on the first take." His face wreathed in smiles told the tale best. "Let's take ten—you've all earned it. Besides, I'm calling an Abby Singer if Bryce doesn't object?" He gave a nod toward the man standing to the side of the set with a clipboard.

The crowd swiftly changed from a screaming beast to a friendly community in a blink of an eye, back slapping, smiles, handshakes all around. I knew an 'Abby Singer' meant there was only one shot left in the day. *Must mean it's a doozey to set up, for being so early —* there was lots of daylight left.

"Good call," Bryce said. Dan gave a look of gratitude to Bryce, his assistant, usually the one to say the happy line on most movie sets. The impeccably dressed man in his pressed pants, white shirt and purple brocade vest responded with the A-Okay, a circle of forefinger to thumb. *Nice. They must be a tight team.*

"Okay, let's check in with the director," Ace said. He ignored the curious glances of cast and crew, intent on his quarry, moving quickly to narrow the gap.

"That was some scene. Doesn't fit the time period. Maybe it's a dream sequence?" I muttered while matching his footsteps at a half-run. I had found it difficult, watching a witch being attacked by an angry mob. It had cut too close to the bone. Our ancestor, my eighth-removed great-grandmother, Mary Sarah Toogood, had escaped persecution in Salem, Massachusetts, by heading due north to Canada in the seventh century. She was the healer I owed my gifts to, with her being the first-born of our bloodline. But there was a catch. My granny had lost her healing gift because she hadn't waited until she was twenty-one to be with her true mate, her one and only. The question remained for me, who was my one? And would I ever find him and be one hundred percent certain he was the man for me?

"Dan Carter!" Ace called out to the lanky director while making a detour past the smoldering pile of wood ash. The man stopped in his tracks, watching us approach with quiet intent.

"Constable Collins, and the young lady from yesterday. Star's sister."

"Charm," I said, filling him in. Of course, Star made more of an impression, *duh*, but didn't mean I didn't wish for a little more physical presence. I pursed my lips as Jennifer's image and her agenda came to the forefront of my mind, wishing again I had been free for dinner on Saturday night.

"How's the investigation going, Constable?" he asked, his brow furrowed with worry. Bryce hovered by his side, clearly ready to run interference if called upon. I so wanted a reading on *that* guy. I inched my way closer, preparing to pounce if the opportunity presented itself.

"It's early days, but we're beginning to get a clearer picture of how the crime happened."

Yes, thanks to yours truly. But probably best not to crow and draw attention to my recent exploits. Another B and E, if one is being fussy. But, it was for the good of the community, so it should be excused, right?

Bryce's expression shifted. Aha, maybe he had a guilty conscience? Then I realized it was because someone else was joining us. Someone he didn't like.

"Mimi," Bryce said, his tone fawning. Ha. *Fake, fake, fake.* I itched to get my hands on him. I scratched at my palm absently, waiting for an introduction, hoping Mimi wasn't a germaphobe as well.

"I'm needing a quick word, Dan," she said with firmness, ignoring the director's assistant as if he had cooties, or worse. She was dressed in a period costume, a long midnight-blue gown, and wore heavy makeup designed to enhance her striking coloring. Thick dark hair in an intricate style flattered her face, and skillful artistry hid the years.

"Mimi, I was just talking to the constable who you've already met, and Star's sister. Mimi Blake, I'd like you to meet Charm McCall."

Please, please hold out your hand. I held out my own with a friendly greeting and smile attached.

Yes. She reached out after a moment and took my fingers, albeit briefly. But long enough for me to catch a glimpse that she had no use for us McCalls, especially one called Star.

I narrowed my eyes at her. Of all the nerve. *Jealous.* That would be a motive for trying to set my sister up. *I'll be keeping a close watch on you, Miss Mimi.*

"Miss Mimi?" a voice called out. Another woman, much younger and bearing a resemblance to the actress, hustled up, her expression worried. The diva turned and gave the younger woman an impatient look.

"Yes, what is it, Felicity?" she snapped, not bothering to hide her irritation.

"I-I wanted to know if you need-needed anything? Water? Juice? Some-something to eat? I p-picked up a ton of your favorite foods from ca-catering and stored them in the refrig-refrigera— Fridge."

Oh, really. So, this was Mimi's daughter. One of the culprits, though my sympathy went out to her for having to live with a stutter. If my food could help ease her pain in any way, then I was the one blessed. I had a sudden urge to try to heal her. Was it even possible? She must have been seen to by experts. Not like her mother couldn't afford to get her all the medical assistance she required.

"No. I'm fine. Really, Felicity, you mustn't hover. I'm perfectly capable of getting what I need."

The young girl nodded, chastised, her expression heartbreaking. She idolized her mother. And the woman was not worthy of it, in my humble opinion. Felicity was a pretty girl and would be strikingly beautiful if she took a tenth of the time her mother devoted to her appearance and applied it to herself. The same thick dark hair but, instead of its style being flattering, it was pulled up into a severe bun. Not even one tendril escaped to add some softness. And her face bore not one scrap of makeup. But she was far prettier than her mother, no doubt about it.

"You must be Felicity Higgins, the poison expert for the movie? I'm Charm McCall, the caterer from the Tea & Tarot café. Nice to meet you." I offered my hand, adding a reassuring smile.

She hesitated, the moment becoming awkward.

"Oh, for goodness' sake, shake the woman's hand already." Mimi's expression was half-annoyed, half-exasperated. Everyone else studiously avoided saying anything, though I did note Ace's expression turning to one of anger. *Yeah, I get it.*

Felicity gulped, her fair skin showing pinpoints of high color on her cheekbones. She reached out, her body posture awkward from her shoulders collapsing in around her chest, like an animal expecting to be beaten. My heart squeezed, pain radiating outward in my chest. Her hand slipped into mine, cold fingers curving around my palm.

Shock. It entered my body as a dark cloud of emotion arose in my mind, transferred from the woman whose hand I held. She was far more complicated than she looked. *Still waters run deep* came to me, another saying my granny was fond of. The fog lifted, the image coalescing into something recognizable. *What is this?*

Chapter Eleven

Felicity was happy that Howard was dead because he had been stealing her mother's money. It looked like a lot of people had a stake in the movie, just adding to the suspects.

She tugged her hand away. Ace shot me a look, and I returned it, hoping my shock wasn't too obvious. Did he know? Was she the one he wanted a reading on?

"Well, if you'll excuse me, I have a movie to direct," Dan said, ruffling his hair back with one hand.

"One more thing, Dan. Are all the trailers set up with escape hatches?" Ace asked. *Hmm, good question. Right to the point.*

Dan gave the Mountie a quizzical glance. "No, not that I know of. What do you mean by that, Constable?"

"Just an oddity we found in Howard's RV."

Bryce narrowed his eyes in thought. I leaned down and pretended my running shoe had become unlaced. I lurched against Bryce when I stumbled, trying to retie it, grabbing onto the director's assistant to steady myself, closing my eyes to get the essential reading.

Uh-huh, oh yeah. I straightened up, letting go of his arm. No love lost there either for the deceased. I was actually beginning to feel sorry for one Howard Smith. Bryce figured Howard was Guido's minion, having too-close ties to the mob with his marriage to Guido's cousin. And Bryce knew about the embezzling. So why had it been allowed to go on for so long? This puzzle just kept getting more pieces added, though it was early days yet. And oh, how my mind loved a good puzzle. At least I had proved that my sister was not responsible — anyone could have done the deed with the accountant, then escaped. A good day's work and it wasn't even supper time.

"Is that all, Constable?" Bryce looked prepared to launch into a hissy fit, his expression full of annoyance at being held up from doing his job. I got it.

"Yes, for now." Ace gave him a firm look and the assistant began to study the ground with interest.

I followed Ace when he walked away from the group. I'd share what I'd learned soon as we got out of earshot.

Halfway back down the trail on my way to Thor, I slowed, turning to Ace. His hair shone dark and glossy in the bright sunlight, this healthy strong alpha male striding at my side. *My oh my.*

"Ace, got a couple of readings. Ready?"

"Always ready, darlin'."

My equilibrium took a tumble, my mouth going dry. I filled him in on what I'd learned, watching him digest my words. Regret about Saturday rose up again, near choking me. I was definitely going to lose out on that one, with Jennifer at the dinner instead of me, darn it.

"Say, would your parents still be around on Sunday morning?"

"Yes. Not heading back until later in the day, last we talked. Why?"

"I make a mean brunch, if you think they'd be interested?"

"That's your one day off. I don't want you cooking. How about we take you out to brunch?"

Nice. "Okay, you're on." I had another thought. "It will be just the four of us, right?" The thought of being a fifth wheel to a family friend — ugh.

"I guess, yeah. But Jennifer could use a friend. She's all alone here in Snowy Lake. She still hopes to spend some time with you while she's around."

Great. Now I looked less than stellar. And just when things were looking up. I had to make this right. I spoke up, hoping I wasn't making the biggest mistake of my life.

"Do you think she has any interest in coming to one of our Northern Lights Coven meetings? There's one tonight." *Who knows, maybe I read her all wrong? There's always a first time for everything. Yeah, and the sun won't rise tomorrow.*

"The same coven that burned me in effigy on the front lawn of the detachment?"

"Uh, yeah, but that was a one-off. They're really just a sweet group of awesome women."

"Sure, if you say so, darlin'." He gave me a quick grin. "Give me your phone and I'll add her number."

I fished it out of my pocket, handed it over then watched him type in a phone number with his large hands that made me long for them to go other places. *Preferably around my body, pulling me in for another one of his awesome kisses.*

"Thanks, I'll call her when I get back to the café. Better reception."

"That's good of you." We'd come full circle now and I was back staring at Thor.

"Well, I guess I'll catch you later. Try not to get into more trouble, please," Ace said, rubbing the back of his neck while giving me a direct look.

"You confiscated my badge, remember, Sheriff?"

"Like that's ever going to stop you."

I reached for Thor's door handle, hoping Ace would stop me, twirl me around and give me a swoon-worthy kiss. No such luck, though he politely shut the driver's door for me after I climbed in. Impulsively, I rolled the window all the way down and reached out, grabbing his warm hand and drawing him closer. When he leaned down, I pressed my lips to his. Electricity sparked between us. *Sweet.* Even my toes curled up from the lovely sensation that danced through me. My, oh my, how that man could kiss.

All the way back to town I hummed a song as I bounced along, working had to steer Thor over the ruts. *"Oh what a beautiful morning, oh what a beautiful day, I've got a wonderful feeling, everything's goin' my way!"*

Just before I made the turn onto Main Street, a person jogging along the side of the road windmilled their arms at me, trying to flag me down. I took my foot off the gas pedal, pulled to the side of the road and braked to a stop just ahead of the figure. A female, by the looks of it, I noted in the rear mirror, waiting for her to join me. Very common to find hitchhikers in our part of the world. Less common to find them so close to town.

But imagine my surprise when Jennifer Morgan jumped into the passenger seat beside me.

"Thank god you stopped!" she said, her voice strained. She gave me a look filled with anguish, her tan face pale.

"What's the matter? What's happened?" I asked, worried for her well-being. We might have been rivals, but that was as far as it went. "Are you okay?"

"I don't know. I guess, sort of." She raised a trembling hand to her head, brushing back strands of hair that had loosened from her ponytail. She turned to me. "Do you know where Ace is at? I need to see him and I can't reach him on my phone. Lousy service in this backwoods part of the world."

I excused her dig at our town. She was upset. "I just left him at Spirit Springs, but I can take you there right now, if you like? Are you sure you're okay?"

She narrowed her eyes at me, her expression becoming more pinched than it already was. "Yes, right now would be good."

I made a quick U-turn in the Jeep, spinning the steering wheel all the way around with my wrist, then heading back the way I'd just come. What on earth had happened? We drove along for five minutes in complete silence except for her heavy breathing, though I kept a close watch on her, wondering if she was in shock.

Parking near the movie set, I turned and announced, "Wait here. I'll find him for you."

She nodded once, her eyes dead serious.

"You sure you'll be okay?" I pressed, reluctant to leave her alone.

"Just find him already," she barked, her lips twitching.

O – kay, roger that. I scrambled out of Thor and began running into the camp past the rows of trailers, spinning my head around, trying to catch sight of Ace while my mind wrestled with Jennifer's verbal assault.

Then I excused it. She'd obviously been through something traumatic.

I spotted the Mountie talking with Felicity Higgins near Howard's RV. He always stood out, head and shoulders above everyone else, his sense of purpose making him shine. When had that begun to happen, him seeming to have a glow around him? Maybe I was coming down with Tulip's gift of seeing auras? Except, his was the only one so far.

I made quick work of running over to where he stood with Felicity. He smiled when he spotted me coming at him, his brown eyes giving me an appraisal that flattered and warmed me to the core.

"And why do I have the pleasure of your company so soon, Miss McCall? Miss me already?" he asked. Was that a wink? My pulse skipped a beat. I wished I was there with better news.

"It's your friend, Jennifer. She needs your help. Right now."

"What? Where is she?" His usual serious Mountie demeanor took over, his plush mouth with the well-formed lips that tasted even better than they looked firming into a straight line.

"Back at my Jeep. I picked her up on the road a few minutes ago when she flagged me down."

"Excuse me," he said to Felicity and, without waiting for an answer, took off running. I chased after him.

When we reached Thor, he went right around to the passenger door and opened it. Jennifer tumbled out and right into his arms, breaking into tears.

Helpless, I chewed on a nonexistent fingernail, working it down to the quick. *Stay or go?*

"Is there anything I can do?" I asked. It was as though one of my sisters was in pain. I so wanted to help. I couldn't imagine what was wrong, and every scenario my fertile imagination came up with looked worse.

Ace turned and looked at me, his expression grim. He shook his head. "No. Probably best for you to just go. Thanks for bringing her to me. I'll take it from here." He led Jennifer across the parking lot to his police cruiser, his big arms supporting her all the way. I sighed, left in the dark.

On the way back to town, I didn't have the energy to sing anything this time. All the shine had vanished from the day.

I parked behind the Tea & Tarot. What I needed most was to get down to some serious cooking and baking to take my mind off things. But when I opened the door and walked into the kitchen, my army of helpers had things well in hand. Maybe having that many hands was going to backfire? They hardly needed me, by the looks of things. They had a splendid assembly line going on, and even managed to look like they were really enjoying themselves.

"Rosalie's waiting out front for you. She's missing an earring her dad gave her and she's beyond upset," Suzanna said, gesturing with a nod toward the public part of our business. I got that. Rosalie had lost her father a year ago to cancer and she had adored him. I needed to take care of this right now.

"I'll be out front if anyone needs me."

A teary-eyed Rosalie got up from sitting slumped over in a booth when I rushed into the front café, my running shoes squeaking fuzzily on the newly waxed floor courtesy of yours truly. I gave her a quick hug, then sat down across from her. The café was empty. Where the heck was Tulip?

"Sorry about your loss," I said, taking Rosalie's trembling hands in mine. Even with her eyes reddened from crying, she looked pretty, with her pixie cap of glossy dark hair and bright blue eyes. "I know what they mean to you." She gave me a wobbly smile. "Just think about the last time you put your earrings on. That would be a great place to start."

"I've looked everywhere, Charm! I've searched the house top to bottom. I can't find it!" A fresh outbreak of tears followed her confession.

"Don't cry, please. We'll find it, I promise. The culprit's got no place to hide from me. You can take that to the bank."

She pressed her lips together to keep the sobs inside, hope gleaming in her beautiful eyes.

"Okay, let's do this."

We both closed our eyes and a vision of her putting the emerald studs with the gold filigree setting into her pierced ears flowed between us. She walked from her bedroom into the bathroom, brushing her hair before the mirror. Aha, the hairbrush caught at her earring, tugging at the fastener in the back, allowing the earring to dangle in a precarious position. But when had it come off? And where? I watched her leave the house and get into her car. Drive to the local hardware, the earring still hanging in there. She parked her car and hurried inside. Why was this taking longer than usual? Normally, I just got an image of where the item had landed — I didn't see a movie of its entire life history.

'Ace, are you intending to spend the best years of your life in this quaint part of the world, for heaven's sake? Without a female to keep you warm on cold winter nights? You know it gets colder here than in Winnipeg, right? Snowy Lake's on the fifty-eight parallel.'

Aha. I knew *that* voice. Jennifer Morgan moved directly into Rosalie's sight line and into the vision we were sharing. Her face was filled with disgust. *Figures.* Then I felt bad, remembering the events of the day, hoping she was doing okay with Ace's help.

Another person strode into plain view right behind her. Howard Smith. That was a surprise. This had to be just minutes before he'd headed over to the Tea & Tarot to get us to cater the movie. So, I was meant to see this. My breath hitched at what had happened to the poor man just hours after this imprint of his life had been captured for posterity. I rested my case on time loops and everything in nature having a distinct pattern. I was right now experiencing the proof of it. Now, if only I could see the actual alteration hours later between him and the killer, this murder investigation would be finished almost before it started. But I could only share the video of what Rosalie and her earring were subject to, and no more. The thread existed between her and the jewelry due to its emotional importance in her life. She'd loved her father and the earrings had embraced that positive vibration.

I saw Howard lean over then clutch at his stomach while Rosalie hovered near by. *'Are you all right?'* she asked him, obviously concerned for his well-being.

He straightened up, a grimace of pain contorting his face. *'Just a cramp.'* He swiped a hand over his mouth. *'Must have eaten something off.'*

He moved out of sight and Rosalie continued, the earring still clinging to her earlobe. The jewelry finally let go, and I watched it turn over and over in a bright sunbeam, shining green and gold, then falling to the tiled floor of the hardware store right behind her. A hand reached down and picked it up. Whose was it?

My pulse sped up, anticipating the big reveal. The hand slipped the earring into a pants pocket. Howard Smith's pocket. Oh dear, this was good and bad. I knew who'd last had it in their possession, but not if he'd left it there, in his pocket, or had time to hide it somewhere else. The trail went cold and I opened my eyes.

"So, do you know now, Charm, where it is?" Rosalie asked eagerly. The hope and desperation in her eyes touched me.

"I know where it last was. And I think we can get it back. I just need to go back to the movie set."

She frowned. "Who took it?"

I filled her in on what I knew.

Rosalie drew circles on the laminate tabletop with her forefinger, listening. "I'm going out there, right now, and demand it back!" she said, her eyes brimming with self-righteous indignation. "I don't care if he's dead. He had no call to steal the earring my daddy gave me."

She slumped, looking unhappy. "I shouldn't have said that. Sorry. Maybe he turned it in at the counter? Didn't take it with him?" She jumped up, full of enthusiasm.

I really thought that a long shot, but all avenues of exploration had to be pursued, of course. "Okay. You check there and let me know. If it's not there, I'll head out to the movie set."

"I want to go with you."

"No, that's not a good idea." I shook my head. "I'll have a better chance at finding it alone."

Rosalie made a face, but didn't contradict me. Then she took off, running at full speed out of the café, headed for Snowy Lake Hardware, the angel wind chimes above the door shouting with maniacal glee. Oh boy, it looked like it would be a futile errand. Well, it did give me time to think.

The time to think was immediately interrupted by Auntie T.J. strolling in, the angels this time announcing her presence with a cautious song.

"Charm! Thank goodness I've found you! Have I got the scoop for you, baby girl," she said, her face alive with information she could scarce contain.

Chapter Twelve

She skipped like she was sweet sixteen again across the floor. Auntie T.J. was a decade younger than her sister and our beloved granny, but the newest intel must be spectacular if she had to see me in person to dish it up hot. I winced, wishing I had not given her such free rein yesterday morning when I was desperate to know the facts about the new girl in town. I generally turn a blind eye to gossip, finding it so often inaccurate. Of course, that wasn't the case with my aunt. She was deadly in the investigating department. Maybe I should thank her for my inquisitive gene?

"Did you hear what happened to that new girl, Jennifer Morgan?" she asked, huffing and puffing as she sat down in Rosalie's abandoned seat across from me, the excitement already having taken its toll. Now she looked her real age, though I wouldn't dream of saying so. I want to keep my head on my shoulders, after all.

"Actually, I just saw Jennifer. Picked her up at the edge of town, then drove her back to find Constable

Collins. She was upset, but I didn't presume to ask why," I said pointedly. "None of my business."

She raised two horrified eyebrows. "Baby doll, *of course* it's your business! Ace Collins is your Mountie."

I sputtered. "He's not *my* Mountie!"

"Well, you'd better look out for your man, mark my words. Jennifer's saying she was just dumped by her long-time boyfriend, Arthur T. Jamison, after turning down a marriage proposal."

"Wait! You mean she was running to Ace because of a breakup?" And here I thought it was because of something happening at the dig on the south side of town in Snowy Creek. The person I'd suspect of seeding it with gold nuggets sat across from me at this exact moment—I was ninety-nine percent certain. Auntie loved a good mystery, plus she wanted more tourists to bring in extra income for the town and café in about equal measure. Not that she would ever, ever admit it. The women in the McCall family had more than their fair share of pride.

"Yes siree, Bob. That's exactly it. Now, that puts a whole different complexion on things."

I frowned, confused. "How so?"

"Well, turns out the reason he was long term was because she won't commit to marriage though he asked her three times. I guess this last time finished it."

"Really, who on earth told you that?"

"I have my sources. And everyone thinks she staged it now because she's after the bigger prize. Your Mountie!"

I didn't bother to correct her this time. I knew Jennifer was after Ace. But she wouldn't be stringing one man along to get another, right? It must have been a coincidence, the broken engagement.

"She's had a crush on him since childhood, you know." She punctuated her remark with a drill of her red-nailed forefinger on the tabletop.

"It's probably all just coincidence," I said, dismissing the charge against the young woman. Sure, she wanted Ace, but who didn't? Half the women in town were enamored at the moment. I could hardly blame her for that. But, to take a law officer away from his sworn duty over a breakup? That didn't sit right.

"And the moon is made of green cheese, baby doll." Some of my auntie's references didn't make a whole lot of sense, but I'd gotten used to such lofty pronouncements.

"Well, I've got to go. Rosalie needs me to find something for her."

"Yes, her earring. I hope you locate it. It means the world to her since her daddy passed."

I gave her a grimace. "I hope so too. She's pretty upset."

"Well, if anyone can, you will."

The unusual vote of confidence from Auntie T.J. gave me pause.

"Thanks. Can you watch the store for an hour or two? I need to get back out to the set."

She looked around. "I hate to state the obvious, but no one's here."

"But they could be, anytime. And my helpers in the back are really busy preparing for tomorrow's lunch and the busy coffee break hour is about to begin. Please, I'll owe you." I stood there, waiting for the cost of the trade.

She gave me a sugar-sweet smile. "Of course, for a night out with our Mountie dancing, I will."

I groaned. "What? Now he's *our* Mountie?" The last time was bad enough when she'd swept him around the Boots & Lace dancehall like a prize bull. "You know I can't promise that. He's got free will. I can hardly circumvent that."

"Maybe. But you'd better circumvent someone else looking to bend him to her will, or mark my words, the deed will be done – signed, sealed and delivered. End of story." She loved punctuating her words, letting them roll off her tongue like the Magna Carta of import.

"Well, if he's set free and doesn't come back to me, was he ever mine in the first place?" I countered, sort of remembering how the saying went. But he had never been mine yet. A terrible sense of yearning and loss struck me, taking me by surprise. I wanted that chance, the time to get to know him, before an interloper cut it off.

"Okay, but don't say I didn't warn you. Women are like blacksmiths – they pick a suitable material and spend years hammering the man into the shape they want, then the guy's a 'keeper'. And if she's done it right, every thought he has after that he will think is his own. And with Jennifer Morgan, you're dealing with a pro, baby doll."

"Maybe," I murmured. "I'll be back soon as I find Rosalie's earring."

I hurried to the kitchen to check on things, leaving the awkward conversation behind. But on one level I did appreciate my auntie's warning. Jennifer Morgan was even more trouble than I had initially thought. And I didn't want a manipulator to get her hooks into a good man. Not if she didn't have his best interests in mind.

On the drive back to the movie set for the gazillionth time that day, I mulled over the facts of the murder case. If Howard hadn't been feeling well before he was struck on the head, had something else been going on? More than just that general sense of unwellness I'd first picked up in him? I would have loved to get my hands on the medical examiner's report as soon as it was completed. I felt the loss of my honorary RCMP credentials, though I supposed it might have been stretching things a bit to suggest they were my ticket in. I beamed all over again, remembering Ace's awesome reaction. He had a grin and chuckle that could light up the world. *Oh yeah, that Jennifer Morgan has another think coming.*

At the camp, I parked then made a beeline for Howard's RV. Before I could reach the former accountant's trailer, Star came storming up. "Where have you been? I've been trying to reach you like forever!"

"Duh, trying to clear your hiney of a murder, run a café, find missing items for people and cater for this lot. All without cell service." I made a wide circle with my hands, embracing the whole location, not even mentioning keeping Ace safe from Jennifer's clutches. At the moment, I was even less in the mood for her diva stuff than usual.

"Why don't you use some of your magic and fix the problem already?" she asked, giving me a raised eyebrow.

"Because it doesn't work! Not on manmade electrical thingies anyway. Now, a human body, that I can do something about. What did you want me for anyway? And why are you dressed like a waif out of a Dickens novel?"

"Well, if you're going to get all in a snit about it. And this is a period costume. I'm supposed to look like this.

It gains sympathy from the audience. At least, that's what Mimi thinks."

"Really?" I snorted. Mimi certainly knew how to keep the shine off those who would rival her for screen time. "Fine, but I have somewhere to be, so if you'll excuse me." I began stomping the final short distance to the RV.

She hurried to keep up with me. "This is something I need your help with."

I kept going, but slowed down a bit, asking in a more reasonable tone of voice, "Okay. What is it?"

"I sort of promised someone you'd do a bit of a healing for them."

I stopped walking. If someone needed my help, that changed the picture. "Who needs help?"

"Mimi Blake."

"Really? What's wrong with her?" My reading of her was she was pretty healthy, physically, if not spiritually.

"Well, it's nothing serious, really, but I thought, since we're working together, you know — her and I — maybe your helping her with a little problem might make the day go better. You know, put some goodwill in the bank."

"Duh, she's jealous of you. That's why she's making your time here more difficult." Now she had my ear and my sympathy. "But first I need to check something. Can I meet you somewhere in fifteen minutes?"

"What are you up to?" She pursed her lips, those beautiful blue eyes locking with mine, calculating, no doubt.

"You want my help or not?" I asked pointedly, not wanting her involved in my sleuthing and being found out. Mimi was making her life difficult enough as it was. Besides, the search would go better without Star messing things up. Star had a way of tossing stuff willy-nilly, leaving a trail of disaster from closet to bedroom door. I didn't need Ace discovering I'd been back to Howard's trailer again.

"Fine, meet me at the catering area. Fifteen minutes, no more. Our break ends soon."

We parted and I stood still for a second, waiting to make sure no one was watching. Then I moved fast, taking the steel steps two at a time and slipping inside the RV. Fifteen minutes later and I was beyond frustrated. No earring to be found anywhere. The trail had gone cold.

Rosalie's tear-filled eyes haunted me as I hurried to the catering tent. Somebody here knew something. And I was going to find that somebody and grill the heck out of them. I had to find that jewelry. I'd made a promise and that I could not break under penalty of 'forever guilt'.

"Finally!" Star grabbed my arm and led me off in another direction, making me feel like some kind of trick pony she wanted to present at court.

She hustled me right over to one of the fancier RVs and up stairs covered by red carpet. Felicity answered my sister's prolonged knocking, inviting us in.

"S-sor-ry, I-I was b-busy," she said.

"Come in, come in," Mimi's impatient voice called out. She was lying against a stack of pillows on a plush sofa, leaving only her jewelled hand with multiple sparkling rings to rise and beckon us over.

I cautioned Star to wait, then strode over to the actress. "Star asked me to help you, so I'm here," I said.

She raised an eyebrow at me. "That remains to be seen if you can do anything."

"Do you want me to stay or go?" I asked.

She shrugged, though her eyes gleamed with interest. "Your sister's been singing your praises all day, so yes, I'm leaning toward letting you do the honors. Though I do hope you are more successful in healing than in being timely. Break's almost over."

Reminding myself that this was a goodwill mission, not a cat fight, I managed to hold my tongue. I sat on a matching ottoman near the sofa and reached for her hands. "I need you to close your eyes and concentrate on what you want fixed."

She gave me a skeptical glance and sighed. "Fine, a mole on my shoulder has been really annoying me and catching on my bra strap. Could you make it fall off or something?"

"I'll check. Just close your eyes."

She gave an eye-roll, but did my bidding.

My vision tunneled, and down into her bloodstream I went, on a crazy carnival ride toward whatever awaited. Nothing looked amiss until I found a dark spot pulsing with energy. Tiny, it was capsulated, but even as I watched, it began to sub-divide into more mottled red angry cells. *Skin cancer.* Certain I was seeing the invader actually start up, I attacked, sending all my energy into the evil presence. I blasted it clear away. When nothing remained, I opened my eyes and broke the connection, instantly feeling a wave of dizziness.

I slumped back onto the footstool, and took a few deep breaths. Tiny pinpoints of light flashed around me like pulsating stars. "That was a close call," I said, swallowing the bile that rose in my throat, threatening to spill out onto the perfect pristine white carpet.

"Why? What did you see?" Mimi asked, her dark eyes round with wonder.

"The spot on your shoulder was turning cancerous." I cleared my froggy throat, and took a few more deep breaths. These healings were not exactly a walk in the park. More like a fight in the underworld with the dragon guardian of Yggdrasil, the world tree.

"Oh, my g-goodness, M-mommy." Felicity rushed past me to grab at her mother's hands.

I looked over at Star, and her expressive face was aghast. "Is she going to be okay?" she asked, her voice trembling.

"I think so," I said. "It was weird. It was just beginning to grow. I guess that's why I didn't sense it earlier today."

"You can tell a person's health when you touch them now?" Star asked, her eyes rounding with emotion.

"Apparently."

Felicity turned from her mother, giving me a smile brimming with happiness. "Thank you."

"Have you looked at it?" I asked.

Mimi twisted to one side so that her daughter could check out her back.

"It's...it's gone."

"Good. You should have a dermatologist check you out anyway," I said. My mind went back to thinking about the earring, the most pressing matter on my agenda now that my work here was completed. An image popped into my brain, the green and gold jewelry at the center of it. But what surrounded the shiny bobble made me startle. Oh boy, this was awkward...

Chapter Thirteen

"A friend of mine, a really nice young girl, lost an earring her daddy gave her before he died of cancer last year. An old family heirloom that belonged to his grandmother. Howard found it yesterday morning, but it seems to have gotten lost since then." I paused, letting the reminder of what happened to Howard sink in. "Do you know if anyone has seen it? It's a green emerald in a gold setting. It means the world to her." Maybe just letting her know the circumstances would be enough to nudge the item from her greedy grasp.

But both women shook their heads, the culprit managing to look mystified. My stomach dropped into my running shoes. *Not good at all.*

"Well, if you do find it, or anyone else does, would you give me a call? The poor girl's been crying her eyes out all day." I laid on an extra layer of guilt called truth.

"Of course," Mimi said, her plummy voice tinged with condescension. If only she knew what her daughter had done—stolen the earring from Howard. Or maybe he had given it to her? But why? If I could just get my hands on it, I'd bet it would still bear the imprint of what had happened but, even more importantly, help heal Rosalie's broken heart.

I got up, the dizziness gone. "Okay, catch you later."

"Uh, thank you," Mimi said, not looking as if expressing gratitude came easily to her.

"You're welcome."

I escaped the RV and took a deep breath of fresh summer air tinged with the invigorating scent of pine and greenery. If Felicity didn't hand over the earring in the next twenty-four hours, I was coming gunning for it.

"What was all that about Rosalie's earring?" Star asked, joining me as I hurried across the lot to Thor.

"The less you know, the better, Star."

"I'm not a child!" she complained, kicking at some loose stones with one shoddy shoe.

"Well then, stop acting like one. I gotta go." Rosalie was going to be so disappointed. The thought squeezed the breath from my lungs. "I did what you asked. You owe me another one, sis."

She frowned, pursing her lips. "Don't forget the meeting tonight with the coven. We're going to discuss a new kind of love spell that Poppy swears by. Oh, and since Christine is feeling great, it's now at her place." A grin popped out. "And I think I know someone who needs a new love potion in the worst way. Just sayin'."

Poppy Spence was one of our founding members of the Northern Lights Coven. If she'd nosed out a new spell, it had to be good. Not that I needed it. Not yet, anyway. *Maybe a cease-and-desist spell for the interloper?*

"I have no need of artificial means to attract a mate, thank you very much." I doubled my strides, managing to outdistance my annoying sister. Okay, protection spells, Kismet Spells and others too many to mention, but a love spell? Not going to happen.

I jerked open Thor's door, then apologized to his spirit, laying a soft love pat on his dash before sitting back and staring out of the window. This week had to beat all. And something else was advancing toward Snowy River, coming in on the fresh breeze just now whipping up over the nearby lake. Something that whispered in my ear about trouble. *Big trouble.*

"What do you call this week? A walk in the park?" I muttered. "A murder, a missing piece of priceless jewelry and a woman looking to hogtie Ace. Send the trouble somewhere else, why don't you?"

I shook my head, then started up the engine and drove back to town. After parking outside Granny's house, I picked up a box of treats I'd packed earlier for her and jumped out. Knocking on the front door sent my mind back to the past for just a brief moment, as it always did when I crossed her threshold. The three of us standing there on the top step in the freezing cold, and my counting to one hundred before knocking — instructions courtesy of my dear long-lost mother. I automatically reached down and rubbed the head of our garden gnome, perched on the first step, for good luck. The gnome's red cap had worn off over the years, giving the impression that he was balding, while heat radiated into my fingertips from the sun's stored energy. *I should give him a fresh paint job.*

"Hi, sweeting. I was just thinking about you." Granny opened the door, her generous smile blessing me. I followed her into the kitchen and plunked myself down at the scarred wooden table we'd all spent countless hours around eating, playing games and, when it came to my two sisters, bickering. But the best part by far was when Granny shared a bit of folk wisdom. Stories about witches or the fae from the old country.

"How are you feeling?" I asked while she bustled about putting on the kettle for tea. By the show of energy, she had to be doing better.

"I'm just fine. Doc's just a worrier. And I've heard you've taken on a large catering project. I should be at the café helping you right now, child."

"Got it covered. If only everything else would go as smoothly." I shook my head.

"Auntie T.J.'s been to see you, eh?" she said, her faded blue eyes giving me a direct look for a split second before she poured boiling water over the tea bags in the china teapot which bore a pretty lavender rose design.

"Yeah, she's on the case."

"Did I ever tell you the story of Great-Great-Great-Grandpa Wilfred's feather and Queen Avallach?" Granny sat across from me, waiting to pour the steaming, fragrant Earl Grey tea into the matching china cups when it had steeped. The one thing my sisters and I had all respected over the years — Granny's tea set she'd brought over from Ireland. *Not one chip, even though they were handwashed daily.*

I shook my head, adding a heaped teaspoon of sugar to my cup in preparation. With the sunlight pouring in through the white lace curtains and the fragrance of Granny's perfume scenting the air with lavender, I settled back in my chair, content to have a break from my own crazy existence. And her stories always had a point.

"Great-Great-Great-Grandpa Wilfred — he was a handsome devil by all accounts and a real charmer with shiny black hair and blue eyes — was courting a woman,

Rowan O'Leary. It happened on a very special night—Samhain. The faeries were out in full force, it being the five hundredth anniversary of Queen Avallach's death. When a faerie queen dies, the web between the two worlds thins and faeries, playful creatures that they are, like to cavort about in our world, knowing they can pull lots of pranks on humans and get away with them. Samhain is an excuse for them to do all sorts of things, because they can make themselves invisible."

"Now that would be an ability I'd like to have," I said, envisioning that awesome power.

"You have your fair share, as do your sisters," she said, with a knowing arch of her eyebrows. "It was time to light the bonfires in the Macalisters' meadow and everyone headed over there. A particularly annoying faerie named Abby was looking to cause trouble with a pair of humans that night and set her cap at Grandpa Wilfred. Well, Rowan wasn't having any of it."

I sat up straighter. "What did the faerie do?"

"She asked Grandpa to dance and tried beguiling him with the act of mesmer. Faeries have this ability to mesmerize humans into doing what they want. And Abby was looking to lure Grandpa Wilfred away to take him to a fairy mound. Time there flows differently—a short while can be years for the fae. Grandpa would have thought he was gone for much longer than he would be, come back all confused and not himself. So, of course, Rowan spoke up and gave her the what-for when she tried her nonsense. Chased her right away. You got to watch faeries, child. Some are good and some are up to no good." She took a moment to pour the tea into our cups.

"Just like humans. Didn't you say something about a feather?" I took a sip of the tea, enjoying its unique ability to soothe and inspire me at the same time.

"I'm getting to that part now. The pair of them were walking home when a shimmering blue feather dusted Rowan's white dress in the moonlight. Probably off a wild turkey — very iridescent and ever so pretty. Well, Grandpa Wilfred picked it up and placed it in his hat and said these very words to her, *'I'm keeping this feather, Rowan, as a reminder of how you set your cap at me on this night. And I've something to ask of you.'* Then he got down on one knee and asked in his wonderfully rich baritone voice, *'Will you marry me, Rowan? You'll make me the happiest man on earth. Please say yes.'*"

"Lovely story," I said. "Not so easy these days to just set your cap at a man. And in my case, it's even worse. If I choose incorrectly — *poof* — there go all my powers."

"Maybe, maybe not." She shrugged, as if she wasn't as sure as the first time she'd shared the information. "Your healing power is the strongest I've ever seen or heard about in all our family's history of gifted healers. Might take more than bedding the wrong man to end it? You have good instincts. Trust them." Granny looked as though she was trying to reason it out or reassure me.

I shook my head. "All the more to lose. What if one of us needed my healing ability all of a sudden? I'd never take that chance."

"You can't live your life worried about *what-ifs*, child. You have got to live your life for you, not by what everyone else needs. Sometimes to find yourself, you must let go, sweeting, come what may."

"Yeah, well, I need a plan just to be spontaneous. Kind of defeats the purpose, don't you think?"

She chuckled, a sound that reminded me of that awesome moment earlier today when Ace had surprised me. "You never did like change. Always needing to control everything and everyone around you. Doesn't mean you can't learn another way."

"Too old." I had a sudden wish that my mother had learned a little control over her drug habit — things might have turned out very differently.

She burst out laughing, then wiped her streaming eyes on her flowered apron. "Charm, don't you beat all? You're twenty-one. You've got a lot of changing to do before this lifetime is over. I look back down on my way of thinking and being when I was your age, and I don't recognize that person now, she's changed so much. Life's journey changes everyone, sweeting, like it or not. Up to you to decide what to embrace and what to let go with each new experience. And if you're lucky, you'll have so many experiences that you'll leave this part of our existence for the next well prepared and ready for it."

"I'm not changing for any man. No matter who it is."

"Don't worry. He'll do most of the changing." She poured us more tea, giving me a waggle of her eyebrows in the process.

"Granny!" I sat stunned by her revelation. I had no idea that Auntie T.J.'s earlier comments about women being blacksmiths ran in the family. I wanted to ask her more, about what she knew about what was next for us, after this lifetime, but something made me hesitate. Some things were better left unsaid. I couldn't see my way past this thing with Ace and Jennifer Morgan, let alone be worrying about the end of my existence on this physical plane. Which didn't mean I didn't have my theories. I took a sip of tea, basking in the moment. I came from an interesting group of women, without a doubt. I set my cup down, another thought coming to me.

"I was sent a message that trouble's coming our way."

"Always going to be trouble, sweeting. Just how you handle it that matters. Remember, all that has been or ever will be has already happened. Life's one endless cycle." She sat back in her chair, a tired look replacing her recent animation. Guilt struck. I relied on her counsel so much that I forgot she was a woman in her seventies.

"I should go. You need your rest." I got up, squeezed her shoulder and gathered up our tea things to rinse them in the sink.

I was kissing Granny on the cheek when the back door burst open and in trooped the errant Tulip.

"Where have you been?" I asked, straightening up and giving her a direct look.

"Aw, Charm, didn't expect to see you here. You must have parked out front. I just came up the alley from visiting with Emma," Tulip said. She looked flustered, handing out way more than enough information. *What is she hiding?*

"Would you like some tea, sweeting?"

"Sorry, Granny, I don't have time. Running late today."

"That you are," I grumbled.

"I just came from the movie set. Have you heard the latest?" she asked, ignoring my dig. She pulled out a chair and plonked down with the smuggest look.

"What's up, child?" Granny asked.

"You'd best be careful or you'll be following in Auntie T.J.'s footsteps," I said, a warning shot over her bow.

"Charm! How dare you compare me to —"

A look from Granny silenced her.

"Anyway, it involves Star so it's *not* gossip. You know that song she wrote to honor our ancestor Mary Sarah Toogood, *The Wailin' Tree*?"

I nodded. "Yeah. What about it?"

Tulip looked fit to burst. "It's going to be featured in the movie!"

"What? No way!" I sat back down. This was beyond huge. Tulip began to sing the song, a decent rendition, though not as tuneful as Star's.

"They haunt these hills, in long white shrouds
A tree stands firm, near weeping clouds
The crowd's long gone, their souls set free
And nobody's left, but me."

I joined in for the chorus while I remembered the long night when Star had stayed up until sunrise writing the ballad after she'd found out what had happened in Salem. It had affected her so much that she'd had to get the deep feelings out by creating the song.

"The wailin' tree, oh the wailin' tree
Nobody's left, but the wailin' tree.
The wailin' tree, oh the wailin' tree
Nobody's left, but me."

Chapter Fourteen

"Kind of a game changer, eh?" Tulip said, her face wreathed in smiles. "Imagine our sister at the Grammy's or even the Academy Awards, the Holy Grail. Maybe we'll all get to go?"

I chewed on my bottom lip. "Yeah, no kidding." Why was my breath tightening in my chest? I had to get out of there, get some fresh air. *Fast.*

"Well, that's incredible news, sweetings. Your sister will finally get the respect and recognition she deserves," Granny said. "A song in a movie—don't that beat all? A granddaughter of mine."

"I gotta go. Tulip, you're on your way to the café, right?" I asked pointedly.

"Yeah, sure, what's eating you? I just told you the best news *like ever*, and you're acting all stodgy. I don't know why the coven is bothering—" She stopped midsentence, a guilty look coming over her face.

"What are they up to?" I asked, hands on hips.

"Nothing. It's not important. Just another spell. Oh, and Emma's going to share what she learned about poppets. Sounds interesting. She's even going to show us how to make one." She smiled, then shrugged. "Okay, I'll go and take care of customers. You go about whatever it is you need to do."

"Duh, there's been a murder if you haven't forgotten? And your sister's been implicated." Her easy capitulation didn't fool me. Tulip was hiding something. *And I'll find out later at the meeting, mark my words.* But making poppets, or spirit dolls as some liked to call them, did sound interesting. That I could get onboard with.

"Nobody in their right mind thinks she had anything to do with it." Tulip rolled her eyes at me.

"Doesn't matter. I have an obligation to our town to look into it."

"Isn't that what the Mounties are for?" she asked, all innocent like. Okay, now I had to get out of there.

"Later," I warned, making a dash for the front door. Outside, I stood on the top step and chewed on a fingernail. *Star. Writing a song for a movie.* The whole thing was too much to absorb at the moment. Time to get my mind onto more immediate things.

I started up Thor and drove to the detachment. *Now to pull a quid pro quo.*

Striding in through the front door, I gave Delores a thumbs-up. She was busy on her keyboard and just gave a quick wave. Then I hurried down the hallway to Ace's office.

Just as I headed in, someone was coming out and I smacked right into them.

"Oops, I'm sorry," I said.

Ace grabbed my arms to steady me and I took a deep breath, enjoying the tantalizing fragrance wafting off him, not to mention his big strong arms that encased me in the kind of protective security a gal only dreams about.

"Hey, darlin', what's the rush?"

"Just wanting to do a little trade," I said. At least he'd managed to somehow escape Jennifer's clutches, something I needed to check with him about. Just not right then.

"Okay, I've got a few minutes. Have a seat."

I slid into a chair in front of his desk, expecting him to head in behind it, but instead he joined me. I wished he had sat farther away, finding it harder to think straight with his melting chocolate-brown eyes endowing me with his full attention. My fingers itched to reach up and smooth a tousled lock of hair back from his face. Would it be as soft to the touch as it looked?

"So, what have you got to trade?" His voice was tinged with traces of humor, startling me from my musings. Was he flirting with me?

I sat up straighter, looking away. "I had an interesting visit with Mimi and her daughter, Felicity, today."

"Hmm, I thought your credentials had been revoked?"

"It was all on the up and up. She needed my help." Why did this man always do that? Make me want to choke him into submission?

"How did you help her?"

"She just wanted a reading."

Ace was not fully aware of all the unusual gifts of the McCall clan and it was probably for the best. Heck, they were still emerging anyway. What would be next? Spinning straw into gold? *Say now, that would be a good one. Keep all my family so well off they'd never want to leave Snowy Lake.*

"Anyway, that's not the point. What I learned from her *is* the point."

"And what is it you want to trade this information for, Miss McCall?" He pursed his lips, one of his dimples flashing into existence, making me want to kiss him again. I sighed inwardly. The guy was just too much.

"Has the medical examiner made his preliminary report yet?"

His eyes narrowed. "And here I was hoping you might trade intel for something a little more personal." He sighed and looked away. "You're too early. Report's not in yet. But I will have to insist you share anything you know about the case, if you don't want an obstruction of justice charge."

"Hey, that's not how this works!"

"It's exactly how this thing works, darlin'."

The phone rang and he got up to answer it while I sat stewing. Even Hannibal Lecter gave a little something to Clarice Starling in return.

"Constable Collins. How may I help you?"

He stood by his desk, dominating the room, listening intently while someone spoke at length on the other end of the landline. My curiosity piqued, wishing I could listen in.

"Really?" Ace's voice changed then, concern clipping the edges. "Of course, I'm on it."

He set the phone back down in the cradle in a brisk move. Opening his bottom desk drawer, he grabbed a thick roll of yellow police tape. I took a moment to enjoy the view of his pants stretching tight over his sweet hiney, then spoke up. "What's going on, Ace?"

He gave me a direct look. "You wanted to trade for the medical examiner's report, right? Well, it's in. I'm heading over to the movie set right now. We can speak on the way."

Was he inviting me along? *Sweetest moment yet.*

I hustled along right beside him out of the detachment's front door and climbed into his cruiser, buckling myself in. Now this felt so right.

"Guess what was found in Howard's system?" he asked, while skillfully driving the SUV out of the lot and onto the street.

"Drugs. He was a cocaine addict," I said without hesitation.

"Yes, but there was something else found of much more import."

My fingers tingled. "What else?" Was this the trouble foretold when I visited Granny earlier?

"Ricin."

Blink.

The word hung between us like, well, like *poison.*

"And he was bashed in the head. Kind of extreme, don't you think? Why do him in twice?" I asked.

"Same question I'm considering."

"Maybe it was taking too long?" I said, speculating.

"What do you know about Mimi and her daughter?"

I gave him a quick rundown on the earring intel.

"Interesting," he said, rubbing his jawline, drawing attention to his handsome mug. Maybe I should have flirted and made a better deal? What would he have offered then?

He parked the vehicle then turned to me. "Wait here. I'm just going to be a few minutes and I need to speak to the director alone."

"I can help," I protested.

"I'm closing down the set, due to ricin. Everything will have to be checked. So, under rule of law, I'm ordering you to wait here."

"What? You can't do that! I mean, that would cost the producers a fortune, not to mention it will jeopardize Star's big chance. A song of hers is going to be featured, for heaven's sake!"

"I'm sorry. No help for it. Provincial standards. We don't know where Howard received the contamination and the lethal doze. A HAZMAT crew is on the way to do field testing. It's probably going to take at least twenty-four hours to clear the set. I imagine one day off from filming won't be too disastrous. Two at most."

I sat back on the seat, crossed my arms over my chest, tapping my toes. Of all the terrible timing. Star was going to be inconsolable if this thing didn't happen. I had to solve this. Now. Then a new thought hit like a ton of bricks. What if someone else had been infected? *Oh, my goddess, Star!* Everyone was always jealous of my beautiful, talented sister.

I was out of the cruiser like a shot, heart pumping and legs churning as I raced toward the sounds of human activity. *Spirit Springs*. It had to be where they were set up today. Full-tilt down the widened path I ran and headlong into a crowd of spectators.

"Shush," a person reminded me as I jostled into them.

"Have you seen Star McCall?" I asked, uncaring of their attempts to silence me.

"No. And they're about to make an announcement. Please stop talking," the young woman hissed at me, shrugging off my hand on her shoulder.

I looked frantically about, then caught sight of the pathetic waif dress. Star. I pushed through the crowd until I reached my sister, ignoring the curses and exclamations of annoyance.

"Are you all right?" I asked, pulling her into a bear hug.

"What? I'm fine. For heaven's sake, let go of me." She raised her finger to her lips. "And be quiet. Constable Collins is about to speak. I need to hear this." She tugged away from me, giving me a strange look.

"Star—"

She took my hand, gave it a squeeze. "*Shush.*"

Fine. Be like that.

"Ladies and gentlemen, if I can have your attention, please," Ace said. My, but his aura was getting brighter. I looked around with curiosity. Strange. No one else had much of one. Maybe because we connected intellectually? And he liked yanking my chain?

"I'm sorry to be the bearer of bad news, but it's been brought to my attention that ricin has been used on set recently and was involved in the death of one Howard Smith."

"What?" Star turned to me, her eyes widened by shock and surprise.

"That's what I was trying to tell you. Howard died due to two things, ricin and having his head bashed in." I gave a head-shake. This would make Felicity Higgins a suspect. Add in the missing earring and the police might have a case. But it was hard to imagine that poor stuttering girl harming a flea, let along poisoning a person. *Kind of too obvious in a way.* She would know that ricin would make her look bad. No, it had to be someone else.

"Good grief. That's awful."

"Well, dead is dead," I said with aplomb. The person standing on my other side gave a gasp. Well, he would have gone through worse if he had suffered a ricin death. Dying from a sudden head bashing sounded less painful.

"Charm, that's an awful thing to say. Poor Howard."

Ace began speaking again, and the crowd quieted down to listen. "Now, due to these unfortunate circumstances, we will be shutting down the production until we can determine that it's safe for everyone. So, if you would please vacate the area until further notice. And, if you are suffering from any flu-like symptoms, please go to the emergency entrance at Snowy Lake Hospital. Thank you."

"Are you sure you're okay?" I asked Star, laying a hand on her forehead. She was cool to the touch, ratcheting down my worry a scant degree.

"I'm fine. Don't fuss." She pulled away from me. "How long will the set be closed, do you think?"

"Just a day or two. HAZMAT can use handheld devices to give a quick check in all the trailers."

"Well, I hope so. Just when I get my big break, *this* has to happen."

"Yeah, I'm sure that Howard is feeling poorly that his murder is inconveniencing you," I muttered. Now who was being insensitive? "By the way, are they going to improve your wardrobe at least, now that you're becoming big news?" I asked, giving a pointed look at her torn and stained gown. I wrinkled my nose. Was it my imagination or did the cloth smell moldy?

"What? I don't know. I gotta go."

"You got a ride?" I asked.

"Duh." She hurried away, rushing toward Ace and Director Dan, where a small crowd had already gathered. *Hmm. Time to ask a few questions of my own.*

I worked my way around the area, keeping a sharp lookout. I wanted to duck and dive Ace for the moment. Steam rising from the bubbling hot springs curled skyward, scenting the air with brine. I loved that smell. How many times as a child had the three of us escaped Granny's clutches to swim in the hot springs' healing waters? A thousand harsh memories had been soothed by their magic. Maybe I should invite Ace for a swim? It sure would beat the week he'd first arrived in town, when we'd both been involuntarily signed up for the dunk tank at the 'Eh Neighbor Festival. Auntie T.J. was responsible for my freezing my hiney off and Ace was the rookie — and all rookies got the treatment. But it had all amounted to the same thing, getting blasted by ice-cold water. Well, it had raised money for a worthy cause, so this buttercup had had to suck it up.

"Well, well, if it isn't the pretty catering lady."

I turned and stared into the face of Guido Morello.

"Mr. Morello," I said, keeping my tone neutral.

"Bad news, this wanting to close the set. Costs everyone more money," he said with a frown. "But maybe it would give us time to get to know one another better, sugar." He ran a finger down my upper arm to underline his suggestion.

"What do you know about ricin?" I asked, moving away slightly.

"Ricin?" He pursed his lips. "Not much. Not the best way to take care of business. I prefer up close and personal, if you get my drift?"

I could imagine him using a knife, or a gun, or maybe even a baseball bat, but poison? Not the mob modus operandi in America. "Who do you suspect?" I asked.

He shrugged. "There's a poison expert on set."

"Yeah, but isn't that a bit too convenient?"

"My money's on someone who has the most to lose or the most to gain. Find them, you find your killer."

But who was that—specifically? Howard didn't appear to have had the goodwill of many on set. All I had been getting were negative vibes toward him. I ticked them off, *Mimi, Felicity, Bryce, Guido, Chace.* Who else was hiding in the woodwork?

"Bryce, over here," Guido called, drawing my attention away from musing about suspects and motives, signaling the director's assistant to join us. The man approached with reluctance, frowning at having been accosted.

"Miss McCall," Bryce said when he joined us.

"Mr. Stanford," I replied.

"What can I do for you, Guido? Things are a bit crazy right now, so I would appreciate your getting right to the point."

"My, my, but things have taken a twist for you. You not worried about the ricin?"

"No, why should I be? I don't have any enemies," he said with a scoff. He was dressed as per usual, his shirt and pants freshly ironed, his hair slicked back and up into a perfect triangle perched on the top of his head.

"Must be nice."

"And what is it you wanted?"

Interesting that Guido was pointing out Bryce to me. Mistrust abounded between the two men. Or maybe he just wanted to show me he had power on set? *Macho thing? So not working.*

"What do you intend to do about this? We can't have the set closed down. Bad for business."

"I'm working on it." He shot Guido a look of frustration that suggested he'd like to do him in.

I laid my hand on Bryce's forearm, feeling an immediate tingle. He was seething with emotion. "Will everyone be okay? My sister, Star, was she exposed?" I asked, concentrating and closing my eyes.

His thoughts cleared at the direct question and he actually patted my hand. "She'll be fine. The culprit will be found. I think there's little danger of anyone else being exposed."

"But how can you know that for certain?" I pressed. Of course, he'd want to reassure everyone to keep the picture on track. It didn't mean anything by itself.

A vision of white powder in a stoppered glass vial and wrapped in cotton batting and encased in wood entered my mind. Was it ricin? And where was it? My body wanted to fire into action, but I hung on, needing more intel. I backed up the picture in my mind to get a bigger bird's-eye view. *Yes.* It was hidden under the floorboards of an RV. And I could easily identify which one. So, Bryce wasn't worried about ricin killing anyone else because he knew where the poison was hidden! Oh my, but he was deeply involved. Did he just store the poison for someone else or had he been the one to administer it? That wasn't clear. But just knowing about the ricin made him look guilty on some level.

Bryce jerked his arm away from my clenching fingers just as I caught him asking himself the question we all wanted answers to — who had bashed Howard's head in? He gave me a suspicious look as if I might be the culprit. *As if, you scoundrel!*

"If you'll excuse me, I have to go," he said in a clipped tone and left.

"So, did you learn anything?" Guido asked, startling the heck out of me.

"What?"

"You have the gift, right? You can see things. My cousin Maria was good at that. What did you find out? Does he have the ricin?"

Chapter Fifteen

I couldn't have been more surprised if an actual bigfoot had come lumbering out of the forest, headed our way. There was a whole lot more to Guido Morello than I'd ever imagined.

I pressed my lips together, holding back a laugh. This was so weirdly unexpected. "Not much really. Just a few cloudy visions," I said as a diversion. I had to let Ace know what I had just found out to stop Bryce from moving the poison to a new location.

"Are you busy for dinner, pretty lady? Seems I'm free for the foreseeable future. Perhaps you might be able to recommend a place a man might stay the night as well?" he asked, blessing me with a cheesy grin he meant to be charming.

"Sorry, all booked up. But if you do want to be of help, perhaps you'd let me take a reading of what you know about Howard's death?"

He didn't miss a beat but held out his hand, closing his eyes. I took it with dread, praying it wasn't a really bad mistake.

"Okay, just let your mind relax," I instructed.

A vision popped into my brain. *Yeah, I know you like me. Move on, buster.* But he seemed more surprised by Howard's death than anything as he showed me images of the last couple of days. He was either a good masker of his intentions, or he had nothing to do with it.

"See anything you like?" he asked as I opened my eyes and caught him staring at me, waggling his eyebrows.

"Well, I didn't see anything that incriminates you, if that's what you mean."

"Never thought you would. Family's family." He shrugged. "No one touches our family and gets away with it." His eyes narrowed dangerously, their dark-brown gleam glittering with intent, his true nature surfacing. "And when I find out who hurt my cousin, Teresa, by killing her husband, I'm not going to let you take a reading on what's going to happen next."

"I think the law is your best bet. You know, being legal," I said. This was getting uncomfortable and I began to edge away from him. He noticed my actions and slipped back into his Lothario role. Better call Martin Scorsese. The guy should be hired as an actor for his next gangster movie — he had it down pat.

"Catch you later, sugar."

Not if I can help it.

I hurried toward the group of people still surrounding the Mountie, sensing I was still being watched by one Guido Morello. I shivered and pushed my way to the front of the crowd. At least I didn't pick up any ill-will toward me from the suspected mobster. He just wanted me to give him some sugar, which was *never* going to happen. Heck, he had a better chance of being a tourist on a spaceship to Mars than getting any 'sugar' off me.

Of course, Ace's look when he spotted me was less than cheerful. His handsome mug darkened with an immediate frown, dimming his aura. "I told you to wait for me in the cruiser, Miss McCall." His tone could have scratched a diamond.

I shrugged, scrambling for a way to share the importance of my information, but not wanting to alert anyone else to what I had just found out. "Gosh, what I've just learned would make the legendary Jack of *Jack and the Beanstalk* happy about his magic beans." Hopefully Ace got the hint and no one else in earshot knew that ricin was made from caster beans. I couldn't exactly tear up the floorboards myself and expose the ricin. What if spores got into the air and I breathed them in? I'd be one dead witch.

"No more questions." Constable Ace cast his groupies to the four winds. *Smart man.*

He hustled over to my side. "I won't comment on your blatant disobedience, but we'll discuss that little matter later." His aura flared with red streaks that would have been pretty if I hadn't understood they meant anger. *Yikes. Stay calm.* "Now, tell me what you know. It just might save lives."

I looked around to see if anyone was watching our interaction. Bryce had vanished. Good — unless he was moving the evidence to higher ground? We'd better get a move on. "The ricin's hidden in a trailer. Under the floorboards. I captured the image from Bryce Stanford."

"You know which one?" Why did he not look more surprised about Bryce?

"Yes. I just need to look around to spot it."

"Good," he grunted. "Let's go."

We hot-footed it together down the logging road toward the camp. People were heading to their vehicles, thank goodness, and not into camp. I strode up and down the row of trailers, looking for the one matching my recent vision. *Yes.*

"There," I said, pointing at the RV with the lawn chairs out front. It looked so homey with the large mat tucked underneath the plastic chairs and matching table. So Canadian. Who had set it up?

"Okay, good." Ace stopped and spoke into the radio transmitter on his shoulder connecting him to the police detachment.

"HAZMAT's on the way," he said after the device had quit crackling and annoying every creature within fifty yards.

He gave me a steady look, making all my senses do a lovely somersault. "What?"

"Just had an anonymous tip phoned in using a burner phone, telling us to look in a trailer that fits this description." He nodded in the direction of the sleek silver-colored caravan. "Someone wanted us to find it."

"Who does it belong to?" I asked. It didn't feel that it was Bryce's. I would have expected a preciseness that was lacking. I savored my victory in having known all this before anyone else did, though I wouldn't be saying it out loud. *Bad manners to brag.*

"Guido Morello."

"No! That can't be right," I said, shaking my head. "Someone must have planted it."

Ace shrugged. "We'll get to the bottom of this. But Guido will have some explaining to do if we find it inside."

"So, what's next? What do you want me to do?" This was all going so splendidly. Maybe I really could have a possible career in law enforcement.

"I wanted to speak to you about Jennifer. Jennifer Morgan."

"Uh, yeah, what about her?" I kicked at a clod of dirt, keeping my eyes averted.

"Ah, she's going through a really rough time right now. Just broke up with her fiancé." He didn't look at me either, the tone of his voice edged with sympathy and something I couldn't place. I itched to put my hands on him, to find out *exactly* what was going on— what he was thinking, but I resisted the urge with every fiber of my being. That was a violation of my gift. I wasn't certain how I knew that right down to the very marrow of my bones, but it was better to be safe than sorry when it came to karma. *Right?*

"Yeah," I said noncommittally, chewing on the inside of my cheek.

He cleared his throat. "She needs my support right now."

"Of course, I totally understand. Say no more. And I should be going, you know, check on the café. Plus, I need to stop at Tuggies and make an appointment."

"Tuggies?" he asked, giving me a quizzical glance.

"Tug's Tire Shop. Thor needs a low tire checked out for leaks. Maybe a rotation. And I should get his brakes checked. Winter's coming in a few months. Be here before you know it and I'll need to have his winter boots—tires installed," I explained. What was I doing? I sounded like a bloody idiot.

"Of course, winter's coming." He nodded, frowning.

"Well, catch you later."

"Hold on, how are you getting back to town? I drove you here."

"No problemo. Lots of people headed that way. I'll catch a ride," I said, walking away as fast as I could.

"Charm, what about that invite for Jennifer?" he called out, but I was already at the twenty-foot mark and moving at the speed of light. Or as close as a human who felt like the biggest fool ever could manage.

I stomped out to the parking lot, taking a quick look around. I groaned, hardly believing my continued good luck. The only two persons left and just now getting into their vehicle were Old Charlie and Tom Ferguson, the bickering hermits that hadn't seen eye to eye since Tom had stolen Charlie's girlfriend decades ago at a dance. Actually, I was kind of surprised they were riding together. Maybe there was hope for humankind after all.

I fast-footed it over to the beat-up, used-to-be-red Ford truck of Tom's, waving my arms and screaming the occupants' names. Neither of the men could hear well since they were both subjected to a vast array of shotgun blasts without ear protection during elk and deer hunting season. It was amazing that Big Red, Tom's old truck, was still on the road, considering the vast number of highway restrictions brought in over the past four or five decades.

"Charm, what are you doing still here?" Tom called out of the driver's window he had rolled down, and waited while I went around and got in beside Old Charlie.

"Just need a ride back to town," I said, buckling up my lap belt. No safety harnesses on a vehicle of this advanced age.

"My pleasure," Tom said while Old Charlie just grunted.

"You not going home with the one that brought you either, eh?" Old Charlie said after a few minutes of silence.

Oh no. This could go south in a heartbeat. At a dance in Snowy Lake, it was only good manners for a woman to go home with the man who'd brought her. And Old Charlie's girl had gone home with Tom that one fateful night a gazillion years ago, never to be forgotten. I'm sure he'd have it etched on his or Tom's tombstone. Or maybe Mavis Skinner's, if he could locate her. The woman had done the nasty then left town for parts unknown. I didn't blame her. This pair would have tried the patience of Mother Teresa.

"Constable Collins had to stay and deal with the HAZMAT team," I said briskly, pretending that the three of us had no idea of the undertow at play. I should have sat between them — less chance of this coming to blows. Though at their age — both men must have been in their late seventies or early eighties — the blows should be less dangerous, right? I just didn't want to get in the middle of an altercation. Maybe a peace spell was in order? This particular thought process took some energy I suspected I should hold on to, considering what this day had already chewed up, but the immediate fix was hard to pass on, whatever the cost.

Hmm, yes. *Goddess of the hearth and home, please aid these two gentlemen to find their way to peace and harmony with each other. Allow your light to guide them…*

Chapter Sixteen

Tom stared at his old nemesis with the oddest of expressions on his face. I just sat there, suddenly too tired to speak, praying that the spell held. My job was done. I needed to go home. If I didn't eat and rest before the Northern Lights Coven gathered tonight, I didn't think I'd be able to make it, my body needing a time-out. *Oh fudge*, I still needed to invite Jennifer.

Tom scratched his head and started up the old Ford, forcing the standard transmission into gear with a loud *thunka-thunka* that didn't bode well. I sat slumped. It would take an earthquake to get my attention in the state I was in. A giant one at that.

"You sure are quiet today, Charm," Charlie said. Tom turned his pride and joy onto Main Street, a giant puff of exhaust smoke heralding our arrival.

"Just tired, Charlie. You coming in?" I asked, when Tom pulled up in front of the Tea & Tarot café, leaving the motor running.

"No, I'd best get home."

"Charm, did you place a spell on me and Charlie just now?" Tom asked, turning his head my way and giving me a piercing look with his faded blue eyes. His scant gray hair was combed flat against his pink scalp, giving him the look of a cherub. A very unlikely cherub, to anyone that knew his past.

"Just a little one to make you both see sense," I said with a shrug. A bit of thanks would be appreciated. *Duh. Not going to happen.*

"I don't need no spell put on me." Charlie puffed up with indignation at the mere suggestion. "Save that rigamarole for those that need it. I know my own mind."

"Okay then," I said and crawled out of the Ford. Every bone in my body ached.

"You sure you're all right?" Tom asked, rolling down his window and calling after me as I did a spectacular imitation of a slug creeping across the sidewalk to grasp at the door handle of the Tea & Tarot.

I waved him off and made my way inside.

"What's the matter with you?" Tulip said, flicking me a glance from her laptop.

"Nothing," I said, shuffling with as much dignity as I could muster across the stadium-sized floor to slump down in a booth. "I just need a quick forty winks."

I woke up to being shaken like a rag doll. I swiped the drool from the corner of my mouth with my hand.

"What's up?" I asked with a giant yawn. I sat back and gave Tulip a grimace. "Why'd you wake me?"

"You have company."

"What? Who?" I wiped the sleep from my bleary eyes and looked around. Ah, perfect. "Jennifer Morgan as I live and breathe," I said, swallowing my mortification at being caught sleeping. Why, oh why couldn't I have an early warning system at times like these?

She stood near the door, looking fine in a pair of khaki shorts and a sleeveless white blouse. And there I sat rumpled, though the catnap had helped. I stretched my spine, grateful that the exhaustion had vanished.

"Charm, sorry for interrupting. I'll come back later," Jennifer said, looking to leave.

"No, that's fine. Join me. What can I do for you?" I reached up and straightened my hair, tucking wayward strands behind my ears. I should have crawled upstairs, tired or not. My stomach growled loudly, reminding me of another basic instinct.

"Would you like coffee, tea, something to eat?" I jumped up and grabbed a couple of blue and white mugs with the fancy imprint of golden stars on them and filled one, looking at her to see if she wanted the other. She nodded and sat in the booth.

"Please, just coffee."

I filled her mug, grabbed a couple of cheese scones, three molasses cookies and joined her. Adding a generous dollop of cream to the coffee, I took a bite of the first cheese scone. *Heavenly.* I polished if off and began on the second one.

I washed them down with coffee, my body finally satiated.

"You were hungry," Jennifer said with a brief smile.

"First chance I've had to eat in hours. Been some day."

"You live quite the life. You're lucky."

"Yeah, I think so. What can I do for you?" I took a gulp of coffee. "Oh, I was sorry to hear about your trouble."

"Ace tell you?" she asked, narrowing her eyes.

"No, but he did ask me to pass this along. Would you like to come to our Northern Lights Coven meeting tonight?"

She shrugged. She didn't exactly look too cut up by the recent break with her fiancé. Ace had done a good job of making her feel better. *Fast work.*

"Maybe. When is it?"

I glanced at the wall clock. Seven p.m. "Ah, about thirty minutes from now." Jeez, where had the day gone?

"Okay, it should prove interesting. Never been to a witches' meeting before."

I didn't like the way she said it, as though we were some kind of group she'd like to put under the microscope. "We're not a witches' coven per se. We just believe in the goddess and doing things that improve the state of our existence, for us, and for others. Being one with nature is healing for the soul."

"Well, nice that you found enough like-minded people in Snowy Lake."

"Yes, very. Would you like to wait here? I need to shower before the meeting."

"Before you go, I just had something I need to ask you."

"I'm listening."

"You've just met Ace, right? Only known him for a few weeks. How do you think he's doing? You know, adjusting to small-town life." She said that as if it must be the hardest thing in the world. *Offended? Not much.*

"He's doing great, far as I know. Fits right in. Now, if you'll excuse me." I caught movement out of my peripheral vision then Tulip was reaching over and giving a swat at Jennifer's hair left loose on her shoulders today, making it fly in all directions.

"Ouch!" Jennifer raised a hand to her head.

"Sorry, you had a *huge* bug caught in your hair." Tulip gave a nod of satisfaction and marched away.

"On second thought, I'll have to skip the meeting. Thanks for the invite, but I forgot I have somewhere to be tonight." Jennifer got up and made her escape.

The angels made a scathing good-riddance sound, but maybe that was just my imagination. I was about to get up when Charlie and Tom came in, surprising me. They hurried over to my booth and sat down, both quite animated. *Hmm, now what?*

"Hey, Charm, I forgot to tell you something," Charlie said.

"Go ahead. I'm running late, but I can take a few minutes."

"Me and Tom were out near Spirit Springs today to look for those darn beavers that are damming Miller's Pond and causing the water to back up into Johansson's meadow, and we ran into some of those movie guys in the woods."

My ears pricked up. "Go on."

"Well, we suspected you'd be wantin' to break the case about that accountant fellow, so we thought we'd better share what we overheard. You know, it might mean something, eh?" Tom said.

"That fancy pants who works for the director, and a couple of guys dressed in coveralls, like stage hands, were arguing. They didn't see us. You know, we're darn good in the woods, hunting and all," Charlie said with a satisfied grin.

"I've heard that," I said by way of encouragement. "And the assistant's name is Bryce Stanford." I couldn't disagree about his fancy clothes.

"So, you've met him. Anyway, this Bryce guy says to the two guys, 'You agreed to it. Now you ask for more!' He was real mad, red in the face." Charlie gave a chuckle.

"Did he say what they had agreed to?" *Ricin*. Maybe the two guys had been paid to plant it?

Charlie shook his head. "No, but then one of the guys said it was risky business and they wanted more money and the other fellow backed him up. The guy, Bryce, wimped out after they suggested they had the goods on him." Charlie pursed his lips, looking more than pleased with himself.

Hmm, could just mean they were working on a dangerous movie stunt and Bryce wanted to keep it quiet. But my gut said they were talking about the poison.

"Thanks. Would you recognize the two men again?"

"Maybe. They had their backs to us the whole time, but I did see that one of them had a ponytail, kind of grayish. The other wore a New York Rangers hat— *backward*." He gave a look of disgust accompanied by a quick Bronx cheer, otherwise known as the raspberry. Tom and I followed suit—the hat didn't belong to our beloved Jets hockey team based in Winnipeg, after all. The whole town had begun doing that regularly since *Corner Gas*, a popular Canadian television show where the whole town always spit on the ground when the next town over got a mention. And wearing a hat backward was almost as cardinal a sin as wearing the crotch of one's pants at one's knees. That one could get the victim tossed in the creek, pants and all.

"Tomorrow, could one of you go out to the set with me if they reopen it? See if we can spot him?"

"I could go, nothin' much planned," Charlie said. "Well, we'll be in touch then."

I watched the pair walk out together, the angels over the door sighing with sweet contentment as they swayed in the breeze, announcing the men's departure.

"What was that all about?" Tulip asked, looking up from her laptop.

"Nothing important. I gotta go clean up."

I left Tulip in charge of the café and headed into the back. The kitchen was deserted, but it was obvious that everything was ready for the morning. That was, if we needed it. What was the deal now that the set was quarantined? I had no time to worry.

I raced up the stairs, my energy restored by carbs, and hit the showers. Twenty minutes later, I tiptoed out of my apartment, not wanting to disturb Ivana. She usually didn't attend our meetings. Why bother her? She had enough on her plate dealing with her crazy Russian family.

"Charm, bosom friend! We go together, yes? I want to learn — what they called? Pippets? Peppets?" Ivana's idea of the perfect outfit for a coven meeting clashed somewhat with mine. I wore a simple yellow sundress with flats, Ivana a tight red lace number with five-inch heels, her hair up in a swirling mass of fire-red curls that would defeat any man's attempt to mess with. Her beautiful face made up to perfection, her bosom heaving from the strain of being pushed up to the rafters, she oozed sexuality like a hound dog howls for the chase.

"Poppets. Spirit dolls."

"Dolls, yes. We make voodoo, yes?"

"Not voodoo. Spirit dolls are to send out into the universe to create good karma for someone, a vehicle of pure energy. At least that's how the Northern Lights Coven will use them, I'm certain. It's empowering. You know, help someone be healed or protected, make a connection between your desire for good, and its manifestation? They can bring great joy to someone you love. You go about making them by saying a little verse, *As I stitch thee, So I wish thee*."

She narrowed her eyes at me, her head quirked sideways. "You use them banish, right? Get rid bad pests?"

"Ah, that's not the best intention for them, Ivana, though in history they have been made for that purpose." I shook my head, trying to dissuade her from such a bad idea. "Not in modern times. Not in Snowy Lake, we don't." I was pretty certain I spoke for everyone in this regard.

"Hmm," she said, giving me a squinty-eyed look. "I use them best. For Charm." She struck her hand over her heart in a closed fist with a loud thump, making me wince. It was her way of signaling that something really mattered to her and was not to be taken lightly. Not that I ever took anything Ivana said lightly. *I'm not that crazy.*

"Good." I hoped she meant to use them to send out good vibrations, not the way she *thought* best, but I couldn't get too focused on making sure or we'd be running late.

"Time to go. Want a ride to Christine's?" I asked, knowing the answer.

"Go best bosom, yes."

"Let's go then." Well, she did have a great set, lots larger than mine, and I was rather endowed.

As I drove Ivana over to Christine's, my thoughts kept circling around the day. So much had happened. What did it all mean? And what else could my gift do?

A deep sense that the whole world was about to open up left me breathless. And spooked. I shivered.

Chapter Seventeen

"Okay, listen up," Emma, my actual best bud on the planet, who was lacking in the bosom department and proud of it—stating she'd be perky at eighty, thank you very much—clapped her hands together to get the noisy group of women to take notice. She looked good, wearing a sky-blue floor-length gown that set off her red curls nearly as spectacularly as Ivana's today. Swirls of gold and purple hues intermixed with the predominant blue of her dress, making the silk appear alive as she sashayed about. I was happy for her. She'd recovered from her auntie's death, put it behind her and taken up skydiving. Apparently, number one on her bucket list. *Mine, catching the killer.*

"Tonight, I'm going to explain the history and purpose of poppets or spirit dolls, then we're all going to make one."

A series of cheers followed her announcement. We'd all had a glass or three of sparkling apple cider, thanks to our hostess. It tasted so good everyone tended to forget it had the same alcohol content as beer. And

Canadian beer is known worldwide as strong beer. I just loved the way the bubbles tingled my mouth. *Not as much as Ace's kisses, though.* I sighed. *Okay, got to keep my mind off that annoying man.*

"So, the first known mention of the word *poppet* in the medieval world occurred in or around 1539. At that time, the name did not have a good connotation, with popular thinking being that they were the vehicles for witches and sorcerers to carry out their nefarious purposes. Of course, they were misunderstood and misused, as most poppets are designed for the purpose of good karma. They have three main uses — healing, attraction and banishment. From making straw dolls for sending troubled or bad spirits floating away on a river or waterway to — "

"Yes, stop!" Ivana held a hand up, her red-painted fingernails poised into claws. "We make straw dollies."

"Yes, great idea." A chorus of women all agreeing with Ivana shocked me. I was more interested in making a doll to protect a loved one, not a straw doll to drive someone away. Or maybe I should rethink that position? No. I shook my head firmly. It was either meant to be or not.

"So, if everyone's in agreement, I'll demonstrate a straw doll first." Emma capitulated so quickly to Ivana's demands that I looked toward the doorway. Had one of her legendary brothers walked in, holding us hostage? *No.* Okay, this was decidedly odd. Why would the entire group be having issues with persons they wanted to banish? At least in my case it made some sense.

Well, I could learn how to create one but not charge it with magic to banish anyone. The example Emma held up was quite cute, making my fingers itch to get started. I accepted the offering of short pieces of straw and cord for binding them together from my friend. I glanced at our hostess, Christine, who was flitting among the women with food and cider offerings with an air of contentment I'd never witnessed before. I crossed my fingers. *Please let her have that child she so desperately wants.* Maybe a poppet and matching baby tucked in a snug cradle would help?

I tuned back in to Emma's spiel. We all dutifully followed her instructions and within the hour a mismatched assortment of straw dolls had been fashioned for posterity. I caught Tulip out of the corner of my eyes handing something off to a few of the women and frowned. I thought I'd caught the glint of golden hair.

"What are you doing?" I demanded, my mind suddenly filling in all the blanks.

"*Nada,*" she said, a smug look undercutting her denial.

"So help me goddess, if you're doing what I think you're doing…" I left the threat hanging. *Much more effective.*

"Charm defend honor," Ivana declared, giving me a scowl and winding a strand of the hair around and around and around the neck of the poppet.

"I don't need defending. If Ace chooses to spend time with another, that's on him. Not me." I crossed my arms over my chest, swallowing against the lump that had suddenly appeared in my throat. "Don't you dare charge these dolls with bad intentions. I'll never forgive you." Of course I would. I wished Jennifer would go away too, just not like this.

"Snowy Creek—now," Ivana said, getting to her feet with a determined look that would easily part the waters of the Red Sea. "Come." Her last word caused everyone to scramble to their feet and troop out after her. I jumped up and followed. Maybe I could neutralize the effect with some good intentions of my own.

It was a lovely starlit evening as we marched the ten minutes to the creek at the south end of town, the air fresh with the scent of late-blooming flowers and bulbs. Snowy Creek stretched in a silvery ribbon highlighted with moonlight for a few winding miles past worked fields and stands of thick forest. *Magical.*

Ivana gave her doll a firm shake, a nasty look, then leaned down and set it afloat on the water. I was relieved she hadn't sunk it with a rock or tied it to a cement block to swim with the fishes. Things were looking up.

"Hidey ho, stripper, time to go!" she said in a booming voice that made a screech-owl, well, screech — which was out of character as they had a range of calls that didn't sound anything like a screech — and fly off in a kerfuffle of feathers and wings.

"Hey, that's not the right verse," Emma protested. *Brave woman.*

But she was right. We'd used that one last month to send a busload of strippers on their way. It had worked, though no actual harm had been intended, as we did raise the funds with a splendid bake sale to fix their ailing bus.

Nevertheless, the other women dutifully followed suit, setting their straw poppets on the water and chanting the silly little verse, led by Ivana. I had to work hard not to laugh. They really did have my back, and it appeared harmless enough, setting the poppets free on such a pretty moonlit night.

"She looks so beautiful in the moonlight."

I whirled around, searching for the source of the words, but couldn't locate them. I shrugged. It must have been my imagination. I got back to business.

A crunch of heavy boots on twigs and stones littering the creek bank woke me to the fact that we had company *just* as I set my poppet free with a hope and a prayer that Jennifer Morgan would get home safely. *Soon.*

"Good evening, ladies," Constable Collins said, tipping his hat. A few southern sighs swirled around me, making me give an invisible eye-roll.

"Evening, Constable," the women said in unison, their tones as smooth as clover honey now.

"Miss McCall, if I could have a word." It was a definitive statement, not a casual invite.

"Sure." I kept my fingers crossed as I followed him back up the shallow creek bed to the road. The last thing I needed was Ace getting wind of the purpose behind this particular event.

"Hey, I found nugget!" Ivana screamed with delight behind us. I studiously ignored the chorus of happy yelps that followed, and continued walking away with our Mountie down the roadway. *Probably just my Auntie T.J. up to her old tricks.*

"What's the deal tonight?" he asked, stopping a few hundred feet away, well out of earshot of my crew.

"Nothing, just a bit of fun. Emma gave a class on making some harmless little poppets and we thought we'd give them a fond farewell." I shrugged it off.

He frowned. "I thought poppets set on water were intended to banish someone?"

Was there *anything* that this guy didn't know something about?

"Not always," I hedged. "Anyway, they were just a practice thing. You know, just to learn the basics. So, what did you want to speak to me about?"

"Well." He cleared his throat. "Jennifer said that Tulip attacked her today in the café."

"What? Are you insane? My sister would never hurt a flea. For heaven's sake, she picks up ants and spiders and sets them free on the doorstep. Drives Star crazy." I planted my feet firmer into the grass, trying to find my harmony with Mother Earth. *Serenity now.* "She removed a huge beetle out of her hair. That's all. Jennifer should be thanking her. Those bore beetles have a nasty bite. Might have taken a chunk right out of her scalp."

"Okay. She may have misread things. She's a bit sensitive right now."

"Yeah, well I did ask her to the meeting, but she said she was too busy."

"Thanks for trying."

Guilt struck. I could have tried harder. *Hmm.* That sucked.

"What's going on with your case?" I asked, ready to share what I had learned today since we'd last talked.

"The pieces are coming together. You're going to find out anyway, so I might as well tell you. We're holding Guido Morello for twenty-four hours. The ricin was found in his RV. Under the floorboards, like you said and confirmed by the tip."

"It wasn't him! I mean, think about it—what does he have to gain? Howard was related through marriage, plus, if you're skimming money, why kill off the man who's helping you to get it?"

"Maybe Howard got too greedy? The mob wanted to send a message? Could be any number of things." Ace shrugged, his handsome face illuminated by the moonlight and making my stomach give a little flip-flop.

"Well, I have some fresh intel." I told him about what Charlie and Tom had overheard near Miller's Pond.

"Thanks."

"Maybe I can earn that badge back," I hinted.

He gave me a look that clearly said *No way in Hades.* "Oh, by the way, my parents had to cancel for this weekend. Something about an issue in the virology lab. Sounded best to take care of that first. They can visit anytime." He shrugged with a smile.

"Yeah, not wanting something released into the atmosphere any time soon. We could all start acting like Pod people or—"

"Or Stepford clones," Ace added with a low chuckle that did nice things to my insides.

"Or zombies. How would you like to go to a wedding?" I asked, before I could change my mind.

"Sounds good. Meet a few more locals, garner more goodwill. That reminds me, HAZMAT gave the green light an hour ago. You're back in business."

"Great. I would hate to see all the work and food prep today go to waste. Of course, we could have donated some of it."

"So, we good here? No need for a Mountie to hang around and make sure your coven doesn't get up to things requiring the law to intervene?"

"No, we're all good. I'll catch up with you later about details for the wedding."

"Perfect. I'm dying to see you in your wedding finery in the Bucket Parade, darlin'."

"Wait! You know about that?" I groaned loudly. Even I had forgotten about it in my enthusiasm to have a partner for the festivities. I hadn't even managed a Graduation date, going with a few of my besties to save face. And we did have a lot of fun, painting our initials on the town's water tower at midnight.

"I mean, if you can't make it, you know, 'cause of work, I'll completely understand." *Not so much if it's due to a certain woman.*

"No, I'm pretty sure I can make it. Unless you're chickening out?" he teased.

My, oh my, the moon was bright tonight. His aura flashed right then and there, nearly blinding me. I looked up. Had the ancient fixture been hiding behind a cloud or something? No, just the same quarter moon as earlier. *Hmm.*

Ace walked away with that animal-magnetism stalk that was his alone, making me wonder what his spirit animal was. Mine was the eagle. I'd spent countless nights filled with dreams of flying over forest and vale, at one with nature, under the canopy of moonlight. I'd have bet, with that noble air, his was the lion. That would explain the need to dominate and survey his domain with such effortless command. I could even visualize a mantle of fur widening his shoulders further.

"Tulip," I shouted out, "I'm heading home." She gave me the universal thumbs-up signal, a wide grin dominating her beautiful face.

I began the short trek back to the café, yawning and kicking at loose stones with the toe of my shoe, thinking about the case and asking for divine guidance. I added a short plea for Rosalie's earring to show up soon. Sitting across from her tonight, seeing her deep sadness, had sucked. I reached into my pocket and rubbed the small coin-shaped bronze disc that I'd had since I was six years old. Given to me by my dad when he had been two months sober, it was the only talisman I had from him from a time I seldom thought about. *Too painful by half.*

Mercies of mercies, I managed to slip into the café without being accosted by any drunken Russians or anyone needing my help to find something or any other crazy event needing my immediate assistance. Or maybe I had this all wrong? I stopped mid-stride in my tiny kitchen, realizing that all these zany events that Snowy Lake was famous for kept me focused on the present and not dwelling on a past I couldn't change.

I took a quick shower, then slipped between fresh sheets, enjoying the floral fragrance of the fabric softener advertised to encourage sweet dreams. Now that would be something. My dreams were too often filled with shadowy figures up to no good...

I woke up groggy, feeling as if I'd been asleep all of five minutes. I checked the clock on the side table. It *had* been five minutes. What had awakened me? A furtive sound downstairs made me startle. *Oops, I did lock up, right?*

Chapter Eighteen

I grabbed my trusty baseball bat from beside the bed, then hefted it over my shoulder and crept from my apartment. The hallway was deserted and I tiptoed to the head of the stairs. I stopped, listening for sounds. *All quiet.* The stairs creaked once halfway down and I froze, worried I had just lost the element of surprise. I took another cautious step, holding my breath, but nothing moved in the kitchen. I made it to the bottom of the staircase and switched on the overhead florescent lamps, flooding the space with light.

I gave the kitchen a quick check. *What is that on the counter?* I hurried over, keeping the baseball bat at the ready. A tiny blue velvet jewelry box sat by itself near the sink. Before I touched it, I hurried over to the back door to check the lock. It was unlatched. I was positive I had locked up. Maybe Ivana had come home and forgotten? I quickly set the bat aside and relocked the door, then picked up the velvet box and opened it.

Oh, thank the goddess. My spirit gladdened when the pretty emerald earring came into view. My guilt-laden plea had worked. First thing in the morning, I'd return it to Rosalie. But who had just set it on the counter? I held the box in my hand, touched the earring with my fingers, closed my eyes and waited.

The image that came to mind was murky. Off-kilter. A stranger had held the box last. Someone I hadn't met yet. Someone whose vibrations were way off the chart. I shivered, a sense of dread creeping down my spine. It was odd, considering Felicity had been the last one I thought had had it. Maybe she'd asked someone else to return it? Did she trust the person enough to take the chance on bringing them into this messy business? I was missing something here. But what? I had more questions than answers.

I closed the box and slipped it into the pocket of my sleep pants and picked up the baseball bat. Back in bed thirty seconds later, I lay against my nest of pillows and gazed upward, hands entwined behind my head, enjoying the view of the florescent stars glittering against the dark ceiling, a project of Star's from years past. I liked it more than I'd let on at the time.

I awoke with the sun, the hard case of the jewelry box jabbing into my hip. I wasn't letting the priceless object out of my sight for one second until I handed it over to Rosalie. I grinned from ear to ear. This was going be one fine day. I gave her a quick phone call and left a message when she didn't pick up.

Hurrying to dress, I jumped on one foot, trying to untangle my pajamas from my leg, then toppled over, the fabric tearing and tripping me up. I hit the floor, knocking the air clean out of me. *Oh – oh. This is a bad sign*, said my superstitious nature, taking over. Whenever I had trouble early in the day, it always foretold worse disasters to come. *Just great.* I gritted my teeth and got up. *Just let your guard down for one second by hurrying to do something and the repercussions could suck.*

A banging on my apartment door made me wince. And here it came. Why, oh why, hadn't I been more careful? I held up my torn pajama bottoms with disgust and sighed. My last good pair, too. I know it was irrational to think my bad karma had anything to do with events unfolding in the universe, but when it happened enough times, a person had to wonder…

I finished dressing, ignoring the persistent knocking until I was decent. Taking a deep breath, I opened the door. Constable Ace Collins as I lived and breathed.

"Morning," I said. My heart did a little happy dance I made efforts to hide. Pursing my lips, I cocked my head to the side, hoping to charm him. "Come to read me the riot act, Sheriff? And how did you get in here this morning?" He did look perturbed and my spirits dropped when something flickered in his eyes. *Yikes.* Had he found out who the banishment poppets were in aid of?

"Good morning, Charm." He touched his big fingers to the brim of his Stetson in that charming way that brought goosebumps to the surface of my skin. "Ivana was kind enough to let me in. Seemed in a hurry to go somewhere. I came to tell you two people are missing. Two stagehands, Sal Colletti and Vinny Taylor, haven't been seen since yesterday morning. Both were expected at dinner last night. And they were overheard complaining of not feeling well by another stagehand, but neither of them showed up at Emergency. So time is of the essence if they're out there and need our help."

The urge to flirt vanished. Two men needed my sleuthing skills. What if they had been infected by ricin?

Dread slithered down my spine again. This was bad if they were sick and incapacitated somewhere in the forest. What Charlie and Tom had shared triggered a sudden thought.

"And one had a graying ponytail, I'd bet. And the other wore a ballcap. What can I do?"

Ace nodded. "Vinny has been described as having that type of hair. Captain Duffy is questioning Bryce right now. Your intel is proving useful. But I was really hoping you'd go out to the camp early and set up something for the searchers. You know, water and snacks. We're going to be asking for any warm body to aid in the search, and it would be helpful if you could be there early."

"You mean a refreshment station?" *No.* I wanted to be in the field, leading the charge. I frowned, knowing of course I'd do it, but I wanted a bigger, more important job.

"Yes, if you could swing it? It would be a great place to gather information as well, I'm thinking. Everyone will come by at some point, right? We all need to eat and drink. The department will reimburse you for expenses, of course."

Yes. Now that was an assignment I could sink my teeth into.

"No need. I like to help out our town." I waved off his idea of recompense.

"I insist. You can't always be out of pocket for expenses incurred by others. You're too generous by half, darlin'."

"When do you want me to get a new reading on Bryce?" *Nice.* I liked being thought of as generous to a fault. It rather lined up with my own version of myself most days. Others, such as how I'd like Jennifer

Morgan to take a hike, did not. I blushed, hoping he'd *never* find out about last night's shenanigans.

"Soon as Captain Duffy's finished his questioning, I'll bring him by the set."

I nodded. "You got time for breakfast before you go?" I asked. "A man big as you needs to keep up his strength." I managed to refrain from batting my eyelashes. *Barely.* Ace brought out so many sides of me that sometimes I had to check my head wasn't spinning.

"Thanks, but I'll have to take a rain check. Captain Duffy's wanting this done yesterday."

"Okay. Well, I'll see you there. I hope they find those men unharmed."

Ace's face tightened with worry. "Me too, darlin', me too."

I followed him downstairs and into the kitchen, enjoying the view. Tight buns, wide shoulders and strong thighs. *Wow.* The guy must work out a lot. And I hadn't even managed to book a fake spray tan.

A sudden knock at the back door drew both our attentions. Ace strode across the room and opened it. *Rosalie.*

I hurried over to greet her. Her cheeks were flushed and she was out of breath, but she had a grin from ear to ear.

"I got your message!" she said. "Where is it?"

"Someone dropped it off last night," I said, pulling the velvet case out of my pants pocket. I handed the earring over, wishing I could have gotten a better reading on it. Was I losing my touch?

Ace gave me a glance, catching my eye. "Who dropped it off?"

I chewed on my bottom lip. "I don't know. They just left it on the counter after I went to bed."

"Didn't you lock up? With a murderer on the loose?" His horrified expression was the perfect example of why I didn't want to get into it. This guy could go from sexy to annoying in a nanosecond.

"It's not like I planned it. Someone must have left it unlocked after I went upstairs."

"You need to find out what happened! To think that you were left unguarded while someone in this town is spreading ricin and bashing people over the head. *My god*, Charm, when I think of what could have happened…"

I crossed my arms over my chest. I wasn't lax in any way. I did lock up. I would have a word with Ivana today, see if she forgot. But I could handle my own affairs, thank you very much. "I'm fine. Let's drop it, okay?

"Fine. But I'm adding you to my rounds. If you hear someone checking the locks at night, you'll know it's me."

"Fine." I rolled my eyes at Rosalie, who flicked a speculative look back at me.

"Ladies." He tipped his hat and made his departure.

Rosalie gave a dramatic sigh, placing one hand over her heart. "I wish someone would check *my* locks at night."

"*Phhht*," I snorted. "Well, I can take care of myself." *How do you spell pain in the butt? A.C.E.*

"I can't thank you enough for finding my earring." Rosalie clutched the velvet box in her hand, her big blue eyes filled with a sheen of happiness. "Can I help you in any way? Return the favor?"

"Constable Collins just told me about two missing men, so I'm going to need all hands on deck to set up a station for searchers right away at the movie campsite. You can help with that if you want?"

"Sure. Just point me in the right direction." Rosalie slipped the earring into her pocket and went to the sink to wash up.

The door flew open and in trooped the usual suspects, Granny, Auntie T.J., Tulip, Star, Suzanna and James. A chorus of *Good mornings* from my crew and my family, then everyone got down to work. When our town called, everyone answered, no questions asked.

In one long assembly line, we went about filling our vehicles with all the food we had to hand. The timing couldn't have been better for being prepared, but I didn't like to think of what the call to action was about. *Two men's lives at stake.*

"Star, Tulip, could you go and purchase cases of water at the Grab-n-go?" I asked.

They nodded and took off in Auntie T.J.'s old Buick with its huge backseat and trunk. Within the hour, we had a convoy of vehicles filled and we set off like one long segmented caterpillar toward the movie set.

Chapter Nineteen

Pulling in at the designated location with Thor, I made a quick perusal of the people gathering— my neighbors. Obviously, the call had been heard loud and clear. The sound of dogs barking in the distance alerted me to the canine unit being called out as well. *Going to be some day.* On high alert, I jumped from my vehicle and half-ran into the campsite with my first armload.

Tension crackled in the air. I handed off my offerings and raced back to my Jeep for more trays. Within fifteen minutes we were set up sufficiently to offer the necessities of survival. Sustenance for body and soul.

I kept an alert eye out for my first targets, that mother and daughter team I didn't trust one iota. The murkiness of the residue of the last image on the earring was a concern. Why? I knew it meant something important, but my mind couldn't come up with the solution. It'd never happened before, so I didn't understand its meaning. Until now, every image had been crystal clear. I could find anything. Any time. I'd built my reputation on that fact. Why was this one time the solution being withheld? Especially since it couldn't be more important. Mulling it over, I almost missed seeing Mimi sashay toward me.

"Morning," she said, helping herself to a basketful of carrot and raisin muffins, popping a half dozen into the woven bag she carried.

"Morning, Mimi," I said. I gave her a bright smile and looked behind her to see if her daughter had accompanied her. *Shoot, nowhere in sight.* "How are you?" She was much more friendly now that I had helped heal her.

"Good." She shrugged. "Though I hardly slept a wink with all this business going on." She leaned in to conspire. Yes, she thought of me as a friend now. *Perfect.*

"Yeah, thinking a murderer is on the loose. Scary stuff, eh?" I watched for her reaction. How worried was she? If she knew or suspected who it was, she'd be less inclined to be frightened.

Her mouth thinned. *Inconclusive.* "Well, not that big a surprise with a mobster on set."

"You think Guido had something to do with it?" I widened my eyes.

"Well, the RCMP do. He's at the station now, you know."

"What about Bryce Stanford? He's being questioned also."

She gave me a speculative look.

"Someone mentioned it."

"No way he had anything to do with it." She shook her head. "He wants this movie to come together swimmingly. He's got a stake in it. I overheard Tom say that the studio's watching. If things go well, he'll get a shot at directing."

"Really? That's huge. What a coup that would be, eh? Getting his own movie to direct."

"Exactly. There's no reason for him to create waves. And he doesn't have it in him, believe me. Bryce is really sweet once you get to know him."

"Well, maybe he wanted things to go smoothly and resented Howard trifling with funds? Bit of a motive there," I said brightly. There was always another side to the coin, and I did enjoy turning it over.

I earned a cold glare for my not-so-innocent suggestion and missed Felicity coming up behind her mother. She didn't appreciate my take on things any more than her mother, judging by the sour expression. *Sorry, but Bryce stays firmly on my suspect list.* Of course, what I knew and what could be proved were miles apart. *For now.*

"Thanks for returning the earring, Felicity," I said in my nicey-nicey tone.

"Wh-what are you t-t-talking about?"

"You're saying you know nothing about it?"

Felicity managed a convincing surprised stare, making me frown now. If it hadn't been her in the café after hours, then who had it been?

A horde of noisy set persons descended on our spread in a hungry wave, taking my attention away. When I had a sec to look up again, Mimi and Felicity had vanished. Granny and Auntie T.J. also took their leave a few minutes later to look after things back at the Tea & Tarot. I suspected my auntie was just looking for an opportunity to fire up her bagpipes and drive away any bad karma that had collected. Well, that and the pesky bears. The wailing anguish of the supposed musical instrument began wafting in on the breeze, confirming my suspicions.

"Charm, oh, Charm," Old Charlie shouted out, waving his arms over the crowd. He elbowed and pushed his way through the assembled people, Tom in tow.

"Morning, Charlie," I said.

"How's it going, Charm?" Tom chimed in.

"Good, thanks. Happy to see you both getting along better. Maybe my spell took, eh?" I teased. "What's next? A spell to make you both forget what caused all the trouble in the first place?"

"And did you also know that Miss McCall's power only stays intact if she remains a virgin?" a voice called out from the back of the crowd. "You might want to make sure she stays away from temptation. Just sayin'."

Oh. My. Goddess.

The bottom fell out of my world. I swallowed, my pulse racing. Sweat trickled down my neck and underarms.

Charlie and Tom looked confused, then turned their heads toward the source of the voice. The crowd parted to reveal the culprit. My nemesis, Jennifer Morgan.

She strolled right up to the table, her expression smug and ever so sweet. "It's true, isn't it, Charm, you have to stay a virgin to keep your gifts? I'd bet the town would hate to lose the one where you can find just about anything gone missing."

I searched for my voice in the maelstrom of emotions invading my body. "That's not exactly correct," I hedged, clearing my throat. "Who told you such a thing?"

"Why, Constable Collins of course."

I pressed my lips together. *Betrayed. Suckered. Devasted.* Those words were not even close to how upset the admission made me.

"Can I get you anything? Some food, or maybe some manners?" Rosalie asked her. She stepped in front of me, nudging me away from the table. She spoke over her shoulder at me. "We need more water. Could you go and get a case?"

I stumbled between the piled cases and boxes of foodstuffs, beyond grateful for any excuse to just walk away from prying eyes, my soul laid bare.

A sudden squawking of electronics sent a high-pitched sound zinging through the air waves. People covered their ears. I recognized the voice amplified by a bullhorn calling for people to assemble at Johansson's meadow. My stomach pitched. Why had he told her, of all people, my most private affairs?

Tears prickled behind my eyelids and it took all my willpower and strength to make my legs carry me out to the parking lot where sanctuary waited. I climbed into Thor's cocoon, slumping back in the seat. I didn't hear the passenger door open until Tulip was sitting next to me. She didn't say anything, just took me in her arms and held me tight.

The tears that had been threatening fell, and sobs shook my body. I let out the pain while my sister held me. A few minutes later and the avalanche of emotions eased, letting some sense of normality return.

"Why would he do that? Tell that woman such personal stuff?" I turned my watery gaze on Tulip who looked nearly as upset as me.

She handed me a bundle of tissues and I mopped up.

"I don't know. Maybe to make her feel better after being dumped by her boyfriend?"

"Well, that just sucks. How can I trust him now?"

She shrugged. "Maybe ask him about it? She doesn't seem to be one with your best interests at heart, you know. She wants Constable Collins all to herself."

"When will men learn that certain women will say *anything* to get rid of a rival? He probably swore her to secrecy. And she couldn't *wait* to tell me. But, Tulip, why did she have to tell the whole town?" My voice broke from the strain. "That's the worst part. I could live with just a few close people knowing. But now — well, guess what happens next. This will spread like wildfire."

"I know, I know. Don't worry, we'll deal with what comes. Like we always do."

I wiped a few bittersweet tears from my eyes.

"Do you want to go back to the café? I can look after things here. Maybe you should have a talk with Granny? She'll understand and probably have a lot better advice to give than me."

Do I want to do that? That was not the image I had of myself. Not the Charm McCall who was a wiz at martial arts and could throw anyone to the mat. I prided myself on teaching a woman's defense course once a week. Oh shoot, Constable Collins was scheduled to visit the group to offer some new moves next Monday.

I shook my head. "No. Absolutely not. Why should I let that woman upset me? I'm going back in fighting. Those two missing men need all the help they can get."

"Great," Tulip said, giving me a thumbs-up. "Too bad the poppets haven't worked, eh?"

"Well, give them time. It's early days yet." *Hmm.* Maybe if I added a new one? I shook the thought away. *Not going to stoop to her level.* "I need to get Bryce

Stanford alone to get a reading. You see him, give a shout out, okay?"

"Sure. I'll leave you to powder your nose." She opened the passenger door and climbed out. "Don't rush. We got lots of help."

"Thanks, Tulip. I feel better."

She blushed and ducked her head down. "You're always trying to help us. We don't thank you enough for that."

My heart gave a monumental rush of sensation. The good kind this time.

We grinned at each other and she departed, taking off in a jog across the lot.

I checked in the overhead mirror and groaned. *Crying doesn't improve what nature gives you.* I dug in my purse for my makeup bag. Pulling out some concealer, mascara and peach lip gloss, I set to work.

Chapter Twenty

Five minutes later I was presentable. I tucked my magic kit away in my purse and slipped it under the seat. Stepping out of the driver's side, I set my resolve to firm.

Back at the catering center, I gave my crew a bright smile. The crowd, including Jennifer Morgan, Charlie and Tom, had vanished since I'd been gone. Everyone must have answered the call to assemble for the search.

Tulip moved to my side, whispering in my ear, "Glad you're here. I just saw that Bryce guy over by that trailer." She pointed it out. I nodded.

"Thanks, I'll head over there."

I took a quick walk toward the area she'd indicated, keeping a sharp lookout. But even after a lot of up-and-down strolls between the trailers, I couldn't catch sight of the culprit. Darn it, he must have gone inside one of the RVs.

The camp was nearly deserted, every able body out searching, no doubt. Then I caught sight of Felicity scurrying between two trailers and made the quick decision to follow her. She headed out of camp while I kept at enough of a distance from her to avoid her catching a glimpse of me, I hoped. But she seemed unaware of anything or anyone around her. She walked with determination at a half-run, taking a shortcut across a grassy field, heading straight for Spirit Springs.

At the mineral waters, she continued, skirting the steaming ponds that gave off a sulfurous odor which cleansed my sinuses in one quick sniff. I stifled a sneeze, my eyes watering. A few minutes later, she headed for Skull Cave. *Oh no. Please, please don't go inside,* I begged. I had a terrible fear of caves. *Claustrophobia.* A largely unchallenged condition because I was wise enough not to go anywhere near a small enclosed space.

I stood undecided while her slight figure vanished inside the dark mouth. But what if Felicity knew something about the men's disappearance? I didn't want to follow her in there. *No way. No how.* I wanted to bask in the summer sunshine, let the cares of this inglorious day fade. Going inside had to be the worst idea ever.

My feet began moving of their own volition toward the looming abyss. I followed her right inside, feeling like the sacrificial heroine in a horror movie. Because what else was there to do? I wouldn't be able to live with myself if I didn't do all I could to help find the missing men.

I shivered in the dank moistness of the oppressive landform pressing down on my tormented brain, listening to the drip, drip of acidic water forming the sharp stalactites pointing down from the vaulted ceiling. My life suddenly felt very, very brief. I mean, one of those huge chunks could fall on my head at any given second. Add the weird sheets of calcite flowing down the walls, distorting and creating odd shapes, twisty helictites creating their own brand of horror going off in odd directions, and it was not a sight to instill confidence. Caving, potholing, spelunking or whatever one called cave exploration — I was still going to demote Felicity onto my 'least favorite person of the year' list. *Just above Jennifer Morgan.* Where did that leave Constable Collins? I had no idea and I refused to go there right now.

Skull Cave did have one thing in its favor — newly installed pot lighting for the movie. I prayed the lights went as deep as Felicity was preparing to descend. While I tiptoed down the awkward and sometimes steep decline toward the bowels of Hades, sweating and mentally cursing my way after my new nemesis, I kept my mind sane by thinking about cave facts. True caves are of the exogene variety, meaning they are deeper than they are wide, and this one snaked through miles underground in the Canadian Shield. It had taken thousands of years for water to dissolve the natural gypsum to create this current monstrosity. The world's longest known cave was Mammoth Cave in Brownsville, Kentucky — four hundred and five miles of scary splendor. *Never checking that sucker out.*

But the single most scary thing about this cave system I was traipsing through was that it ended under the sea, which was covered in ice during the winter. Some brave souls from town even went down there through ax-hewn ice-holes to pluck oysters from the ocean bottom while the tide was out. *Now tell me any sane person wouldn't find that worrying?* I wiped away the trickles of sweat sliding down my forehead with the back of my hand and licked the salty residue off my upper lip, praying for salvation. *Like Felicity instantly deciding to abort her mission.* No such luck. I pressed my lips together to avoid screaming and continued my progress.

The slight sounds of rubble being disturbed by Felicity's feet kept me on track for direction, though so far there was just one way to go—deeper and deeper into purgatory. Hellfire, the bottomless pit, netherworld, whatever one called it, I just wished the nightmare would end. My spirit animal wanted to fly free, not creep through nasty caves that smelled of dank sulfur and bat dung. I slipped and fell against one side where the channel narrowed, my hands pushing against the rough, chilly denseness of the rock to right myself, scraping my palms. I rubbed my hands against my upper arms and swallowed the sharp pain.

The pot lighting ended abruptly, signaling I was in even deeper do-do. To continue following Felicity, I would have to get closer to her fleeing figure moving like a wraith ahead of me. Then she switched on a powerful flashlight. A brilliant move in hindsight. *Ha, another rhyme.* Maybe there was hope for my song-writing skills to blossom in the future. *Or not.* But if she turned that sucker of illumination toward me, I'd be a deer caught in the headlights.

Should I turn back? The dilemma didn't stop my feet from moving forward. They seemed divorced from my thinking, because any sane person would have given up this mission. I wanted nothing more than to exit this cave for the great known. *Right. Freakin.' Now.*

Then it got even better. The cave forked. I hesitated while Felicity trekked down the smaller alley, her flashlight eerily announcing her progress and making the ancient landform demons grin at me with evil intentions. Chills swept up and down my spine. Bony hands looked to reach out, pull me against them and never let go. I let out a shaky breath, trying to stay focused on the need to find the men, but, oh boy, spooky was not something I did well.

Then the light vanished and my whole body shuddered.

Where had she gone? I couldn't see a darn thing ahead of me. I waited, afraid of falling in the darkness and alerting her to my presence.

Ah. There. A faint glow pooled near the floor. She must have stepped into an opening off one side of the main tunnel. Was this a Mexican standoff? Was she waiting for me in the darkness? *Crap.* If she had been involved with Howard's murder in some way, I had just caged myself in with a killer.

I made myself take one small step, then another. I crept up to the spot I had last seen her, pretty certain I was certifiable. I leaned forward just enough to see around the corner. *There.* She was in an alcove that went about forty feet back into the rockface, talking to a man in the darkness. A darkness that did not hinder me now, my eyes having had time to adjust.

He slipped something into his pants pocket. He was tall and didn't fit the description of either of the missing men. Who was he? I hadn't seen him around the set before and he wasn't dressed like a local.

"I'll call if things change. But right now, we can't chance it. Too many eyes watching," Felicity said in a crisp tone, the acoustics good enough for me to hear her every word.

What was different about her? *Yes.* She wasn't stuttering.

I stayed in place, excusing my eavesdropping by the larger needs of the missing men.

He gave a mock salute. "Okay, but give some warning, babe. I can't pull this stuff out of thin air. Gotta give my guys some notice."

She gave him a quick glance then turned and began to walk out of the indent in the rockface that had created the small room.

Okay. I had to get out of here.

I stumbled over something and caught myself. I picked up an object in the shape of a hat. Holding the item, I hurried away as fast as my two feet could carry me back in the direction of the entrance. There was no way to avoid her spotting me, now that she was behind me with a flashlight. No time to waste.

Suddenly wolf howls resounded.

No. I froze.

They called from somewhere deeper in the cave. Maybe. Sound was hard to pinpoint underground. Cold sweat poured from me and my throat tightened.

More ancient calls followed the first. Echoes penetrated my brain until it was roiling with fear. My worst nightmare. Wolves.

Move — now.

My feet finally got the command and my legs began working again, sending me careening down the narrow corridor.

I scrambled out of the entrance of Skull Cave, never once turning around to check if any person or creature was close. I'd seen enough movies to know that was a trap. *Trip and it's all over.*

And a flashlight would make a useful weapon in a pinch, if Felicity harbored any ill-will toward me for spying. I just kept moving in the direction of camp, my legs pumping, my eyes squinting against the sudden shock of bright sunlight. Of course, I had my karate moves if it came to that. I could take her down if need be. Unless she was a black belt too? But wolves, that was an entirely different matter.

I didn't stop my forward propulsion until I was back at the catering station. Thank goodness Tulip was still in evidence, busy refilling the trays of goodies. *Safety in numbers.*

She gave me a close look. "What have you been up to? You look odd. All sweaty and everything."

"Nothing." I let out a deep breath. I looked down to inspect the object I held in my hands that I had ignored until now. I excused the oversight—I'd had a few things on my mind.

"Look at this, Tulip! It's a New York Rangers hat."

She gave the obligatory Bronx raspberry. I automatically joined in—we had our traditions to uphold. Then, eyes closed in concentration, I gave my full attention to finding any vibrations on the ballcap.

Yes. A clear image of the man who it belonged to came into my mind. I opened my eyes. "The two men are in Skull Cave. We need to alert the authorities. Right now!"

"You went into Skull Cave?" Her voice rose to a high pitch. She was fully aware of my and Star's condition, a legacy left over from childhood. Add to that getting lost in the actual cave overnight just months after coming to Snowy Lake, and I was pretty much a basket case in confined spaces. Until today. I had gone inside, faced my fears and I now held proof in my hands. *Goddess, please let their lives be spared,* I prayed.

"Yeah, I was following a suspect I thought might lead me to the missing men. You coming with me? We need to find Captain Duffy."

"He took out a search party. They'll be miles away by now. But I saw Ace a few minutes ago."

I winced. The last person I wanted to see. *Put on your big-girl panties, Charm McCall. The two men come first.*

"Yeah, I know, it sucks after what that piece of work Jennifer went on about." Tulip's mouth formed into a straight line while her eyes got a steely gleam that didn't bode well for the geologist. It might mean more than poppets this time.

"Where did you see him?" I asked, ignoring her words. I didn't want to discuss what had happened earlier.

"I'll show you. People can help themselves to what they need."

We set off at a trot. I kept a sharp watch around, expecting Felicity to confront me over my spying at any second. She hadn't been far behind me.

"Who were you following that made you go into the cave?" Tulip's blue eyes rounded with interest while we ran side by side. "I still can't believe you did that." She shook her head in disbelief.

"Well, turns out Felicity doesn't stutter all the time." Maybe she only got stressed around her mother? And that made her stutter?

"Felicity Higgins? What does she have to do with it?"

"She was the one I followed into Skull Cave."

"Really? What was she doing there?"

We had made the parking lot. I could see the police cars lined up, with a few people milling about. Ace was one of them. Not hard to find with that darn spotlight thing going on around him. *Reminder to self – ask Tulip if that's how she began seeing auras? One at a time?*

"Felicity?" I asked, my mind blanking.

"Yeah, who else we talking about? You okay, sis?" She gave me a concerned look.

"Yeah, just peachy." I clutched the hat in my hands and made myself march right up to the small group.

"You might want to look at this. It belongs to one of the victims. It's a New York Rangers ballcap." I thrust it at him.

Everyone except for our constable gave a Bronx raspberry.

"What's this? An episode of *Corner Gas*?" he asked with a quirk of his lips. *Clever man.* Most of us had the grace to look chastised.

He took the hat from my hands, frowning. "Where did you find this?"

"In Skull Cave, near the junction. The two men are a bit farther down the tunnel." I had a clear vision of the pair lying on the cave floor, barely conscious.

"Can you show me?"

I swallowed hard. Last thing in the world I wanted to do was to go back inside. "Okay." My tone sounded hollow even to me.

He gave me a searching look, the question obvious.

"Not too fond of confined spaces," I said.

"Yet you went in there once already today?" His brows knitted together, tighter. He looked good. He wore his Stetson at a jaunty angle, his uniform impeccable except for the residue of dust and pollen around the bottom of the legs from walking through fields. His brown eyes shone clear and bright with that sexy-intelligence thing he had going on. I'd never have known that he had the ability to betray a confidence just from looking.

"I was following a suspect. Didn't pan out," I said in a clipped tone. It wouldn't be fair to mention Felicity until I knew for certain why she was there. And losing a stutter wasn't a crime. With a mother who overshadowed her like Mimi did, it made sense that she would find life stressful. But I would keep an eye out, just in case, because it was an odd thing to have done, met a guy in a cave when two men were missing. Maybe she was a drug addict? And the guy was her connection? But then why hadn't I picked up on that before?

"You okay?" he asked.

Tulip gave a snort. I silenced her with one sharp look. Not the time.

"I'm fine. Let's go. But you need to be aware I heard the howl of wolves inside the cave." I turned abruptly and began to lead the way back down the road. I was getting my wish, to be directly involved in solving the case. But the stunt Jennifer Morgan had pulled rankled, a sharp burr digging into my sensitive skin. And thinking about Ace's involvement — well, I just couldn't go there.

The small group followed us. At the mouth of Skull Cave, I hesitated.

"Okay, before we head in. Susie..." Ace pointed at Susie Diamond, the owner of the Clip Joint. The very woman I had been wanting to make a tanning appointment with for days. I shrugged. Why bother? Not like I was trying to impress the Mountie anymore. The thought hurt more than expected. "You head back to camp and round up more volunteers and a paramedic or two. Tell them to bring stretchers and blankets. And to hurry."

Susie nodded, her golden and pink curls bouncing around her shoulders, the front held back by a sparkly barrette. Susie was a big woman, plump and in charge. Everyone loved Susie. She knew how to make a woman look her best, at any age, any event. At least I had managed to nab a coveted hair appointment for Saturday morning before the wedding. *Not sitting in a tractor bucket without some style.* Good hair, according to Susie, was certain to take center stage, give a woman the edge. I needed all I could get. Maybe pile it high like Marie Antoinette. Or not. *French Revolution ring any bells, Charm?*

Then I gathered my resources and walked under the rock overhang above Skull Cave. I felt Ace watching me from time to time, but I blithely ignored the looks. The sooner I showed him the spot, the sooner we could part ways. Tulip kept close to my side, her presence a great help in keeping me focused.

At the junction where the cave took two separate paths and the light fixtures ended, Ace pulled his flashlight from his black leather belt and turned it on. I walked a short distance ahead of him. "I found the ballcap right here." I pointed to the ground.

The foray into the cave this time had gone better than expected. It seemed I'd lost my acute phobia at some point today, which didn't mean I was giving up blessing the constable with the stink-eye. Or three.

"Okay, let's move it," Ace instructed.

We hurried down the tunnel that narrowed with every meter of ground covered, single-file, the flashlight heralding the way. We went by the spot where I had watched Felicity and the stranger have a conversation.

"It shouldn't be far now," I said. *Please, please, let them be okay*. If it was ricin, there wasn't any guarantee that, even with the best medical care, their lives could be saved.

The team walked in silence, each person no doubt focused on what we would find.

"There!" I half-shouted when a prone body came into view, lit eerily by the searchlight. I began to run, pushing past Ace to get to the man's side. I leaned down, cradling the man's head on my lap. He moaned.

"He's alive!"

Ace handed the flashlight off to another searcher and crouched beside me.

"Will, can you hear me?" he asked.

The man moaned again, his eyelids fluttering.

"Who did this to you?" he asked.

No answer. The man remained prone, continuing to moan softly. A couple of the men scurried by us, moving down the tunnel in search of the other victim.

"Over here," one of the men shouted from a short distance away.

Ace got to his feet. "Stay with him," he said. He hurried off to check out the other man.

"You're going to be okay, Will." I whispered my mantra over and over, praying it would be so. Could I help him?

Poison was a different commodity, I soon discovered, laying a hand on his chest. The toxin had spread everywhere, affecting all his organs. It would take a miracle to save the man. But I had to try. I went in, challenging the enemy, blasting at every damaged cell with laser focus. Bright lights flashed inside my brain, sparks flying like someone welding in a workshop, visible behind my closed eyelids.

Amid the chaos ensuing around me, I kept my focus keen. I wouldn't let go, sensing this man's life could be saved if I gave enough of myself. Chewing at my lips, sweat dripping in my eyes, I swallowed my fear of losing myself entirely. I had to keep the faith that I would recover. I kept at it until my head swam with dizziness, my limbs cramped and my stomach roiled with nausea. Certain I had done all I could, I stumbled to my feet. I had to help the other man.

No one stopped me as I lurched the short remaining distance to the other prone body. I slumped to the ground and laid my hands on the victim. The paramedic moved out of my way. I didn't take the time to ask why. Ace stayed nearby, remaining silent, while I made my journey inside.

This man was even sicker, his organs pulsating with lethal poison seeking to liquidate its host. Without a thought, I began the process all over again, sending all the healing my body could muster into the man's system. I was young, my health strong—surely it wouldn't kill me?

Again the tugging and pulling on my spirit, but harder to bear this time. Pain sliced through me. My mind spun in a drunken way, faster and faster. Armed with ammunition that I sensed could fail at any time, I kept the faith. Kept pushing at the enemy, trying to decimate the poison, the roaring in my ears deafening. I had to save him. No one else could. *Please, please, let me save him.* I pushed harder. Took the pain.

Then the power ended. The laser focus vanished. My body crumpled forward, reduced to rubble.

Hands pulled at me. "You have to stop, Charm. You're hurting yourself."

Too late.

I distantly recognized the voice. Then my mind went black, and I felt myself falling, falling, falling…

Chapter Twenty-One

I had blanked out. I came to and found myself being carried in a pair of strong arms, cradled against a broad chest. I huddled against the warmth, breathing in a fragrance that filled me with a wondrous sense of security. *Weak as a kitten* was an expression I now understood. *Too well.* But I was still here, alive, and I knew the men were, too.

I would have reached up and touched Ace's grim face if I could have found the strength. He sensed I was awake, though, and looked down at me. His gaze collided with mine, his dark and worried.

"Where are we?" I croaked, stirring a bit to see if my limbs were still attached. My whole body ached, as though I had gone skydiving and forgot to pull the ripcord before hitting the ground. *Head first.*

"Just about out of the cave. Now be quiet, you need to rest. You scared the bejesus out of me, darlin'." He pulled me tighter to him, and the primordial drumbeat in his chest pulsated against the side of my head. *Thumpa. Thumpa. Thumpa.* Reassuring and wonderful.

A terrific sense of being home overcame me. Of being where I belonged. It was a shame we were almost out of the cave—I'd missed most of this glorious journey, with being unconscious.

Even when we made the mouth of the cave, he didn't put me down, but continued carrying me as if I was as light as air. An ambulance was already present, and the two men were loaded in, both speaking and talking to their attendants and looking immeasurably better, from the brief glimpses I managed.

Ace strode across the ground toward the camp, his energy seeming boundless. I could have suggested he put me down. I was better, drawing surprising power from just being in his arms. But why rush? Each second that ticked by made me stronger, the pain receding and vanishing by the time we made the parking lot.

Realizing I was playing possum at this point, I spoke up. "I'm quite capable of walking now, Sheriff."

"I'm taking you home. Captain Duffy can handle things for a while." He tucked me inside his SUV and prepared to buckle me in, but I just shook my head and did it myself. Cocooned in the vehicle, I sat buoyed by a sense of contentment I didn't think I'd ever quite experienced before. Maybe when I'd made something yummy to eat and everyone was happy? Nah, that didn't even come a distant second.

People with avid expressions of interest on their faces swam by the window like a child's kaleidoscope. I would have some explaining to do. *Later.* I sat up. Ace had some to do right then.

I slanted my eyes at him and cleared my throat, an image of Jennifer Morgan rising in the mists of my mind like a vengeful spirit. If anyone needed a full raspberry salute, it was her.

He gave me a quick assessing look while turning the wheel of the police cruiser onto the road that led back to town. He'd taken off his Stetson and the late-afternoon sun glinted in the side window, bouncing off his thick dark locks. *Keep your mind on business.*

"What is it? You okay?" To his credit, his tone was filled with concern.

"I'm fine. But I have a problem with you — a big one." I crossed my arms, letting out a puff of air in exasperation.

"Before you say anything, I want to apologize."

So, taking the wind out of one's sails was a real thing. *Who knew?*

"O — kay."

It was Ace's turn to clear his throat. "I heard what Jennifer did today. What she said. I'm sorry that happened to you. It was wrong of her to draw that kind of attention to something I told her in strictest confidence."

"Why did you tell her?" My jaw clenched. "There's no earthly reason. I'm not here to amuse *her*."

"I'm sorry, it wasn't like that. It slipped out when I was trying to make her feel better. Give her something to take her mind off her troubles." Ace ran an aggravated hand through his hair, disheveling the shiny locks in a ridiculously charming way.

"You shouldn't have told her. Three people can keep a secret — if two of them are dead."

"Ah, wise words from Benjamin Franklin. I should have listened. So, I'm now on your hit list?" He gave me a rueful smile.

"Maybe." I pushed my lips out, contemplating the state of things.

"It won't happen again. You have my solemn promise."

"Okay. I accept your apology. But I'm placing you on probation, Constable, just so you know."

"Acknowledged and accepted." He nodded, his expression shifting. "What's going on with you? What I saw in the cave—I can't explain. One minute I thought the men were dying, and the next, you did something and they revived? What's that about?"

I let out a deep breath. "I seem to have come into another gift. Healing the very ill."

He shook his head, his expression confused. "How's that even possible?"

"I don't have a clue." I chewed on my fingernail, not certain if I could explain how I did it. It sounded crazy to me, and I had been there.

"That's some gift, darlin'. When did this start happening?"

I looked out of the window. We'd made Main Street and the Tea & Tarot was close by. "Just recently."

"I don't like what it does to you." He shook his head, his plush mouth pressed into a grim line. "You passed out in the cave. It scared me half to death. I don't think you should be doing something that takes such a huge toll on you."

"What? You want me to stop doing what I'm supposed to? Stop making people better? Because that's not going to happen, Ace, not now, not ever!" My anger and worry spilled over. He'd pulled up in front of the café and I jumped out, ignoring him calling my name.

After slamming the vehicle's door, I stomped off, beyond annoyed at the turn of events. Sure. I got the worry. Heck, honestly, I was worried too. So much was up in the air. But when called, a person had to answer, even if there was a cost, right? *No ducking and diving responsibility. Not on our family crest or motto.* I did a double-take, suddenly reminded of a cold reality. My parents had abandoned their three children as though we were trash. The hurtful thought just made me angrier.

I sighed. I still didn't know who had administered the final death blow to the hapless accountant. Hopefully the two men we'd saved today could supply facts that would help end this case.

Curiosity replaced my anger. Stepping inside the Tea & Tarot, I found a small group of people assembled.

"What's going on?" I asked, furrowing my brow.

"Charm! There you are!" Auntie T.J. scurried up to me, her expression animated.

"What's going on?" I asked. Was there a meeting I'd forgotten about? It did explain, however, why Ace had had to park so far down the street.

Auntie T.J. leaned in and whispered, "They're here to see you, baby doll."

"Me? What on earth for?"

"Everyone needs a little something fixed or found. The talk's getting out about your helping the men in the cave today." My auntie fussed with my hair, pushing strands behind my ears. "You look like you could use a bit of a fix-up." She gave a big sniff, her nose twitching. "And maybe a shower."

"Look! There she is!" a loud voice called over the small crowd and heads turned my way. *What the fudge?*

"Charm! Me first!"

"No! I'm first!"

I did the only thing I could think of.

I ran.

Down the street I sprinted. All the way to Snowy Lake Hospital three blocks off Main Street at the far end of town. I turned into the curved driveway and raced down the sidewalk toward the front electronic doors. Inside the air was cooler, calmer, and I stopped to gather myself, feeling embarrassed and guilty for having abandoned everyone.

Hmm. While I was there, I might as well check on the two men. I stepped up to the front desk and gave Stacey Evans, the receptionist for the last dozen years, a big smile.

"Hey, Stacey. How are things?"

She frowned at me, her perfect brown bun pulling so tightly on her face that she'd given herself a facelift. She'd better be careful — that could lead to noticeable hair loss. "Why are you out of breath, Charm? And all sweaty? Do you need to see a doctor?" The look turned to horror. "You weren't exposed to that poison — ricin — were you?"

"No. I'm fine. Just running. I wanted to see how those two men are doing? You know, the two just brought in that were found in Skull Cave?" Out of the corners of my eyes, I caught some movement. I instantly recognized the guy. Chace Wilde. What was he doing here? Now was my chance to right the omission of not finding him sooner to get a reading.

"Let's see." She turned to her computer screen and punched in some info. "Yes, they're still here. Room 107."

"Thanks."

I turned and bumped into Chace hovering behind me.

"You're Charm McCall, right?" he asked. He smoothed a hand over his short brown hair.

"Yeah." I held out my hand. "Nice to meet you. I'm sorry about your friend, Howard. I wish I could have helped him."

He took it reluctantly. What? Another germaphobe? Or did I look that sweaty?

"Thanks. I heard about what you did today. For those guys in the cave." His Adam's apple bobbed up and down as he spoke. Nervous. Why? Maybe because I'd done something a bit off the map today? I had an instant visual of all the people waiting at the café. *Oh boy. Don't think about it. Maybe the problem will go away. Yeah, and maybe pigs will dress in tuxedoes.*

"I did what I could," I said, shrugging.

"I guess your gift doesn't work after the fact." His voice drifted off. "You know, after they're dead." His face got wistful. "I wish you could bring him back."

"Who? Howard? He's been dead for a couple of days." I shuddered at the dreadful idea.

"Ever heard of the *Monkey's Paw* or Stephen King's *Pet Sematary*, Chace?" *Yikes.*

Chace looked so downcast that I leaned forward and hugged him. He was so sad, so filled with a sudden rush of hopelessness at my words.

"I'm sorry. I wish there was something I could do, but, I'm afraid it's much too late now." I pulled away with a shudder I couldn't hide. The guy was like a black hole, sucking in all my energy.

"I'm sorry too," he muttered then wandered off.

I felt his pain. He was really broken up at his friend's death. Why had he been so angry at Howard that day in the café? I'd probably never know, but I understood that Chace needed closure. And I was fairly certain he hadn't killed his friend.

I hurried down the hallway to room 107, pushed open the door and slipped inside. *Shoot.* Ace was standing near the bed, talking to the men. Everyone looked up as I entered.

Ace appeared frustrated, as if he wasn't getting answers. *Good.* I pasted on a smile and ventured closer.

"Hi there," I said, adding, "I'm the woman who found you."

"You're Charm McCall, right?"

I nodded, moving to the side of the bed of the first man, ignoring the fine strapping Mountie I was still angry at. The guy with the gray ponytail was sitting up, his expression guarded, but I could tell he was pleased to see me.

"How are you doing?" I asked. It was obvious that both men were fine, but I wanted their goodwill. We needed answers.

"Fine now, thanks to you. You're our guardian angel, sweetheart. You saved our lives, you know. I thought me and Will were goners for sure. I'm Sam, by the way."

The man in the other bed nodded, his expression grateful.

I shook my head. "Nice to meet you. But I'm no angel. Just glad you're okay. Very happy about it in fact. My goodness, who did this to you? Who poisoned you?" I reached out and touched the man's rough hand lying against the white hospital blanket, grasping it tightly in sympathy.

While he pressed his lips together, shaking his head, a vision of what happened appeared in his brain, a virtual video of recent events. He blamed Bryce Stanford. They'd hidden the ricin in Guido's RV at Bryce's insistence, receiving a tidy sum of money for the job. They'd been in the cave later on to meet up with the PA to be given more cash to keep them quiet. Now he was worried about repercussions, going to 'lawyer up' to avoid being found guilty of impeding justice and committing crimes.

I nodded at Ace. I had this. All of this, now that I had Bryce's motivation clear in my mind. Seeing him earlier with the director Dan Carter, working on the movie set so cozily, had told me the why of it in a flash of brilliance, if I did say so myself. Bryce coveted what Dan had.

"You know, there's one way to thank me for saving your life — just admit who did this to you. Send the culprit to jail where he belongs. There's not a doubt in my mind that Bryce Stanford tried to kill you both. He'd been promised a chance at directing his own movie and wanted to stop Howard from stealing the funds to make the current movie go smoothly. Then, when he needed a likely scapegoat, he had you both plant the evidence on Guido. He doesn't deserve your help, now, does he?"

The man's eyes widened, filled with awe and wonder and confusion.

"How did you know all that?"

"My job — albeit self-imposed — is to find such things out for the sake of our town. Please, your part in this affair's nothing compared to what Bryce did. We need to stop him, put him in jail so he can't poison anyone else. The whole community's at risk, not to mention your movie family. And I'm sure, with your testimony, something can be worked out. Right, Constable Collins?"

I spared him a glance, daring him to disagree with anything I'd just said. And since I had such an appreciative audience, I added, "And furthermore, I'm sure you'll find the evidence you need in his walking stick." I shook my head. "I should have seen that earlier. He borrowed a page from the Russians who favor an umbrella for such events."

Ace twitched but didn't object. "Okay, Miss McCall is quite correct. Getting the murderer locked up — priority one. The part you both played was of far less importance than Mr. Stanford. I'm certain we can look into reducing your charges or offer you a plea deal if you testify against him."

Ace looked right at me, giving me a proper nod of recognition for my part in solving the crime. *"Well done, darlin'."* An instant connection, almost as though I could hear his thoughts of approval, flowed over me like the warmest ray of sunshine. I wanted to bask in it, but the other half of the puzzle awaited.

Who had bashed Howard's head in? It wasn't Bryce. Why, after Howard was already a dead man walking? Someone who didn't know that, of course, but also someone else who had a lot to lose. Money and/or jealousy being the usual motive. Someone unbalanced by anger or greed. Who had a lot to lose and was also unreliable, unpredictable? Why I'd had so much trouble reading Rosalie's earring suddenly made a whole lot of sense.

"Okay, well, I'm out of here," I said.

I dashed from the room, not wanting to be stopped before the finish line.

Chapter Twenty-Two

"Miss McCall. A moment of your time." A loud booming voice should have stopped me in my tracks. Not this time. I kept hotfooting it along the corridor, headed for freedom.

I didn't make it. An abrupt end came to my march mid-strike when the big hand of the law planted itself on my shoulder. Happy chills I decided to ignore raced through my system. I had no time for this — a murderer was still on the loose.

"Why are you running away from me?" he asked. His tone held a twinge of hurt.

I rolled my eyes. *Like you don't know.* "Just got somewhere I need to be."

He gave an even bigger sigh. "I do believe that's my job, Miss McCall, keeping the citizens of Snowy Lake safe."

"How can I make it up to her? I'm so sorry I said anything to Jennifer."

"My trust is not easily given, Sheriff." I shrugged. "It has to be earned back."

"I must find a way. She means so much to me. And I don't want to see her hurt trying to help others with her talents and gifts. She's one in a million."

"What can I do?" He pulled off his Stetson, ran a hand over his hair, then dropped the hat back into place.

"I mean a lot to you?" I said, surprised he'd just come out with it. "One in a million?"

"Yes, of course. But how did you know?"

"You just said so!"

I looked him in the eye. His eyes widened, confusion followed.

"I didn't say that out loud."

"You did. Just now." I stood in shock, staring at him.

"What's going on here? Did you just read my mind?" His expression shifted to horrified. *Uh-oh.*

"Think something else, something I could never know."

He remained silent, waiting for me to pick up on his thoughts.

A vague impression was all that came, try as I might. "Something about Shakespeare's family?"

"A quote. *A touch of nature makes the whole world kin.*"

"Hmm, nice. But I didn't get all that." I experienced a touch of disappointment, one I ignored. I had a sudden inspiration. "But if you do want to help me, go clear out the mob at Tea & Tarot." Okay, I was exaggerating a tad, but two birds with one stone was hard to pass up.

"What's going on at the café?"

"Everyone seems to need something from me today. Tell them to take a number. Or better yet, make an appointment. They have my solemn promise I will get to every one of them as soon as I can." Then I remembered his warning and concern for my well-being. But it wasn't me who'd started this problem, made it public. Oh goddess, another thought crept in, scaring the stuffing right out of me. But I had to ask.

"Ah, can you hear me if I don't say it aloud?" The last thing I wanted was someone to hear *my* private thoughts. Ling Ling, okay—we had a decent mental connection that I made more of than actually existed, but that seemed rather normal. She'd be described as my familiar in old-fashioned terms in another time, another place.

"Not sure. Think something." I had his full attention now, his brown eyes liquid pools of intensity.

"Oh boy. What to think? Ah, sure is a weird freakin' day, eh."

"Sorry. Not getting a thing."

Thank you, goddess.

He scrubbed his hand down his face, his chest rising and falling with his deep breaths. I swore I could hear a bell tolling somewhere. Soft voices spoke near my ear. I cocked my head to listen, but they were too faint to understand. Maybe a radio or television was playing somewhere? We were in a hospital.

"Telepathy's mentioned in *Real Magic*, that book I gave you. And I've heard of people knowing something just before it happens, like going to the phone before it rings or avoiding a plane or car trip when sensing danger. But I'm grateful that we don't fully share it."

"Me too."

"I think we need to talk more, though," he said. A muscle jumped in his cheek.

"Just check out the café, please. Catch you later, Sheriff." Then I got the heck out of Dodge, one twitchy step at a time.

"That's a promise you'd better keep."

I ignored the parting shot and kept moving. I sensed him watching me all the way to the end of the corridor before I turned left and walked out of the hospital. When I made the street, I took a moment to get my thoughts in order. I needed to pick up Thor and head to the movie set.

Not thinking it wise to be seen until I had the crime completely solved, I took an old shortcut between some houses and businesses, skirting Main Street then slinking out of the back of the café to hurry into Thor. Turning the key, I started his motor and we set off.

Excited, knowing this could prove useful or a complete disaster, I parked and scurried into the camp. Distant sounds alerted me to the production steaming ahead again even in the aftermath of the men being rescued. *Time's money, right?*

The camp remained eerily quiet while I made my way toward the catering area. I soon discovered that Tulip, hopefully with some help, had packed up all the remaining food and drink and gone home. *Good.* This whole thing with the movie people had consumed far too much of our time and energy. I sighed, wishing the film was in the can.

Okay. Might as well go for broke. Squaring my shoulders, I knocked on Mimi's RV, the metal door rattling under my rapping fingers. I waited, listening for any sounds from inside. *Hmm, nothing.* I knocked louder a second time, bruising my knuckles in the process. I shook off the pain just as the door opened.

Felicity stood in the doorway, her sleepy face explaining the slowness to answer.

"Wh-what do you w-want?" she asked, her tone quiet and meek.

"I was wanting to have a word, if you have a few minutes?" I snuck a glance behind her but saw no one else.

"Now?" She yawned.

"If you could. Is your mother in?" Mimi had money invested in the movie, which gave her a motive as well.

"No, she's fil-filming. They are be-hind."

I nodded. "Yes, crazy doings lately. But thank goodness the men were found safe and sound. Can I come in?"

She reluctantly moved aside, and I squeezed past her through the narrow doorway.

"I h-heard you helped th-em." She plonked down on the sofa. I sat down next to her, my thoughts racing.

"Yes, fortunately, I found them."

"How d-did you kn-ow wh-where to look?"

"I followed you."

Her eyes widened. "Really?" Her innocent look appeared real, not put on. Were my suspicions off base?

"Yes, I found the hat. The New York Rangers hat." I didn't make the usual raspberry salute. It seemed wrong under the circumstances, with what I suspected to be true. "I saw you speaking with a tall man. You exchanged something."

Her eyes narrowed with the intel. "You go wh-where you sh-shouldn't go. Not nice."

"Well, it did save the two men's lives," I reminded her. "And now the murderer has been found out. The PA, Bryce Stanford."

"W-why are y-you here then?" she asked.

"I thought you might know something. Something you're not aware of. I thought perhaps I could take a reading on you."

"But you al-already kn-know who did it."

"Just wanted to tie up some loose ends. Like who returned Rosalie's earring."

She looked confused and innocent again. "If you th-think it h-helps."

"Oh, it will."

She let me take her hands and I went to work, but nothing was revealed, just a foggy mist that swirled and didn't amount to anything. I needed to be more direct. "It wasn't just Bryce who murdered Howard. Someone else bashed his head in. In a way, he was murdered twice. A dead man walking. A shortened version of Christie's brilliant *Murder on the Orient Express*."

The woman startled, tried to pull her hands away, but I held on. "Please, it might help," I murmured.

"I think you've done quite enough already, Miss McCall."

Now we were getting somewhere.

Chapter Twenty-Three

I continued to hold Felicity's cool hands while images flowed into my mind. Crystal clear this time, of Felicity bashing Howard over the head with a baseball bat. Felicity running through the RV and shimmying down the escape hatch and away from the trailer. Felicity madder than a hatter.

I opened my eyes, swallowing hard. The person previously known as Felicity had changed in that few scant seconds. Her eyes no longer held any trace of innocence, but a murderous gleam. From Doctor Jekyll to Miss Hyde. Time to get out of there, tell Ace the score and get back to figuring out my newly complicated life. And in exactly that order.

I pulled my hands away from hers. "Okay, well, thank you, you've been an enormous help."

"I have, have I? Just what did you see, Miss McCall?"

"Just that you returned the earring. Thanks for that. I'm sure I can speak for Rosalie in sending along her best regards." *Please, please buy it.*

"Hmm. I think you saw a lot more than you're letting on."

I squirmed in my seat, my skin crawling with the sensation of jittery ants. Maybe I'd better send out an SOS, just in case. I closed my eyes and brought an image of our new Mountie to the forefront. Man, he sure was a looker. *"Calling Constable Ace Collins, I'm at Mimi's with Felicity. If I go missing, tell my family I love them."*

Okay, here it went, the moment of truth. I gave Felicity my fakest all-is-hunky-dory look and got to my feet. "Well, I'd best get a move on. I've got to prepare the food for tomorrow's catering. Anything special you'd like to have us prepare, Felicity? Chocolate's a house specialty."

That disarmed her for a second before she squinted her eyes at me. "Why are you calling me Felicity? I'm Eve." She slanted her head at me, her eyes assessing. "You seem nervous. You okay?"

"Oh, sure, I'm fine, thanks, Eve. Just a bit overwhelmed with the extra workload this week. Catering for a hundred and fifty is, well, a hundred and fifty percent increase."

She shook her head slowly. "Yet you found the time to snoop all over the place for missing people and follow me around. And yes, I visited the cave to meet up with my drug dealer, if you must know. Kill two birds with one stone. Find out just how interested in me you were. Did you know that cocaine's not readily available in Snowy Lake? You're all so darn provincial in this hick town. But something's not ringing true, missy. You had no call to follow me. No reason other than you're a busybody looking for glory."

I inched my way toward the door, keeping a wide smile pasted on my face while ignoring her slanderous comment on our fine town with great difficulty. I didn't want to spook Felicity/Eve. Now I understood why I hadn't picked up on the drug use before. Until now when I'd taken a reading, she'd been Felicity, not Eve. That was some split in her personality. *Right to the core.* "I blame it on my obsession with Agatha Christie and her passion for solving mysteries. I guess it's catching."

She got up as well, planting herself between me and freedom.

I braced myself. If a person couldn't run away, which should always be considered first in a dire situation, then fighting was the only option.

A whirlwind of movement and a baseball bat appeared in Felicity/Eve's hand, grabbed from behind the sofa where it had been hidden from view. She was still obstructing my leaving, only now she had a weapon in her hands. And a look in her eyes that chilled me to the core.

"Feli—Eve, it's my duty to warn you I know karate and the art of self-defense. And I practice a lot."

She grinned, holding up the bat as though she was ready to play ball. "Bring it on, missy."

A flash of movement. I instinctively ducked out of the way, my body filled with adrenaline. *Surprising how fast you can move when your life is being threatened.* But the space was tight, hampering me. *And did I mention she has a thick wooden baseball bat?*

We circled each other like beasts in the forest searching for any weakness. Any opening.

Please, a little help here.

She took a second swing. I dodged out of the way. Not quick enough. A solid blow smashed into my arm

on my left side, firing up all my pain receptors. *Shoot.*
That was going to leave some bruise and I had a
wedding to attend this weekend in a strapless
bridesmaid gown. That was, if I lived through this. I
swallowed hard. Those kinds of thoughts—not
helping. I crouched into defensive mode. Enough of
this. *My turn, sweetheart.*

Of course, all I had was my own body to use as
leverage. I went for broke. Rushed her, screaming my
battle cry—it was best to go down fighting.

"HI-YEEEE!"

It knocked her right onto her boney hiney. She landed
against the door with a loud thud, effectively blocking
the exit. I fell half on top of her and rolled away
immediately. She looked dazed, but not out of the
game.

Not yet.

She still clutched the bat. She brought it up again with
both hands in front of her prone body, intending to
strike. I tried scrambling farther away, but my back was
against the side wall, the sofa blocking my other side.
Yikes. I directed all my energy at the weapon, wishing I
could shatter it to smithereens.

A loud crash reverberated against the outside of the
RV. She bounced against the door, her eyes widening.
The bat wobbled precariously in her hands. She
struggled to hold on to it, but it seemed to have a life of
its own. The weapon flew out of her hands, bouncing
once and rolling away.

A second crash made her scramble away from the
door on all fours. I stayed still. Good thing, because
there was a third crash and the door flew open.

Constable Ace Collins, poised like a superhero, gun
drawn, stood in the entrance.

My adrenaline plummeted, my body recognizing instantly that the danger had passed. I began shivering with cold. It had been a whole lot too close for comfort.

"You okay?" he asked me while holstering his gun and striding over to my attacker. He hauled her to her feet, placing her in handcuffs. I got shakily to my feet, holding on to the sofa for support.

"I think so," I said, gingerly checking my arm to see if it was broken. I pulled up my sleeve. *Uh-oh.* It didn't look good. Or feel good. Already swelling like the dickens. "Ah, then again, maybe not. I think I might have to have this arm set."

Ace's expression darkened. "Stay right here. Don't move. I'll be right back soon as I lock this perp safely in my cruiser."

I slumped back to the floor, overwhelmed.

I lay there, listening to the sounds of the RV. Nice and quiet with a single clock ticking the heartbeats away over the compact refrigerator. Nice. I could lie there all day and...

I woke up being cradled in a strong pair of arms. My nostrils flared with the now familiar scent of our almost-new Mountie. The fragrance of leather and man wafted off Ace in spades. I took a deep satisfying breath, filled with contentment, the pain in my arm receding. Yeah, but how soon until I was ready to tear a strip off him again? My relationship with him confused me. Was it even a relationship? *We haven't even been on a proper date yet!*

"Twice in one day. We must stop meeting like this, Sheriff."

Ace looked down at me. He shook his head, his expression grim. He tucked me into the passenger side of his SUV before answering. "I'm taking you straight to the hospital. You need to have that arm looked at. And perhaps an MRI of that stubborn head of yours, see if the doctor can't locate some common sense."

"Yeah, well at least now you've got all the murderers locked up, thanks to yours truly," I countered. *What, ten seconds of bliss followed by anther annoying outburst? New record.*

"I am not the annoying one here, Miss McCall — "

"Take me to jail already." A voice interrupted from the back cage of the police vehicle. Presumably Eve's. No stuttering. Real small-town stuff, a victim and perp traveling together. Not that I'd ever been a victim, at least not any more since I'd grown up and could defend myself, thank you very much.

"Eve?" he asked, giving me a quizzical look.

"Yeah, Felicity goes by two names," I said. "And how did you know that? Something you're not telling me, because I won't put up with your not being honest with me! Just spit it out already."

"I'm not holding anything back. If I want you to know something, have no fear, I'll just come out and say it." He closed the passenger door and went around the front of the cruiser and got in the driver's side. "Anything that can be done if this thing becomes more of a problem?"

I shrugged, gingerly cradling my arm. "Sorry, no spells in the Northern Lights Grimoire for releasing thought sharing. At least I don't think so. Of course, never experienced it with a human being before." I leaned back against the seat.

I chanced a glance at him after a few moments of complete silence. He was nonplused by my comment, but I could see the twitch was back under his eye as he stared straight ahead at the road.

In short order we made the hospital, and leaving Felicity/Eve in the backseat of the cruiser, Ace escorted me inside.

"Miss McCall needs to see a doctor right away," he barked at Stacey. I laid a hand on his arm, rock-hard muscles cording and bunching through his uniform shirt under my touch.

"It's okay, I'm going to be fine, Ace." I tried soothing him, recognizing I was somewhat responsible for his current state of being.

I addressed Stacey. "I think my arm's broken. I may need an X-ray. Is Dr. Tanner on duty? He's our family doctor."

"Of course, Charm. Just have a seat and I'll give him a call." She frowned at the Mountie hovering at my side and picked up the house phone.

I led the way over to a line-up of plastic orange chairs facing the desk and sat myself down.

"It's okay if you go and see to Felicity now. I'm in good hands."

Ace looked undecided, an expression that endeared him in the moment. "By the way, thanks for showing up when you did. You get my message?"

"I was already headed to the camp, so I was close behind you. No mental telepathy to blame for that one. I just know you. Can't keep yourself from charging ahead, no matter what the cost. I've decided to find it charming."

"Oh, yeah." I gave him a smile. I could live with that diagnosis.

"Charm McCall," Stacey called out. "Dr. Tanner will see you now."

"That's my cue. And don't leave here. I'll take that woman to the detachment and be right back. You hear me?" He leaned in close, took my chin in one hand, tilted my head back and planted a sweet, lingering kiss on my lips. A tingling sensation zinged its way right to my center before he stepped back. *Oh my.*

"Aye, aye, Captain." I gave a lazy salute with my good hand and watched him stride away. That darn halo of his was getting brighter. If he kept this up, I'd be blind soon. But at least I had forgotten my sore arm for a few precious seconds.

I made my way slowly to Dr. Tanner's examining room, wincing from the pain that jarred with every step I took. I needed more kisses — they seemed the best medicine at the moment.

"Charm, strange to see you here. What on earth happened?" Doc Tanner looked up from behind his desk where he was writing notes on a chart. He observed me holding my arm propped up against my chest. His craggy, still handsome face creased into a network of wrinkles. He loved the outdoors and had come to live in Snowy Lake over thirty years ago for the hunting and fishing. Everyone was glad to have his competent help, and the fact that he was dedicated to our town didn't hurt. The only time I actually ever saw him was at town events. I never got hurt or sick. *Until today.*

"I got hit with a baseball bat." I made a rueful face.

"Accidentally?" he asked.

I shook my head. "No, it looked kind of deliberate."

"Who on earth would do that to you?" He was scandalized, by the expression on his rugged face.

I shrugged. "Doesn't matter, really. But I think it's broken."

"Best let me take a look at it. Have a seat." He got up and came over, carefully taking my arm and gently feeling along its length. "It's badly swollen, so a break is a real possibility. We'll get this X-rayed right away. Don't worry, we'll have you fixed up in no time."

"Where's my sister? Charm? Where are you?" A loud series of voices erupted from outside the examining room. The door burst open, and there stood Tulip, Star, Granny Toogood, Auntie T.J. and my best friend Emma. Behind them I could see a sea of Northern Lights Coven members' faces.

"We heard at the café what happened! That you were attacked."

"My goodness, are you okay, sweeting?" My beloved granny's voice made the tears well up. I shook them off.

"I'm fine. Or will be, once we get this sucker X-rayed." I held up my wounded wing, trying not to wince.

"Was it that wicked Felicity Higgins that hit you? I'll bet it was — we saw her in the back of Constable Collins' cruiser," Star asked, her expression taking on the proverbial *loaded for bear* demeanor.

"Well, yeah, I think the poor woman's a bit off, if you know what I mean. Possibly the result of a terrible childhood. She was calling herself Eve and not stuttering, a sign of a split personality." I sensed if I didn't calm this crew down, the burning of Ace in effigy on the front lawn of the detachment might not be anything in the historical record of our town compared to what these strong women were capable of if they thought one of theirs was treated poorly.

Tulip crossed her arms over her chest, not buying it. "Well, we all did, the three of us—had a terrible beginning to our lives before Granny took us in. Didn't make us grow up to hit people with baseball bats.

Howard Smith's dead and I'd bet it's because of her."
Her eyes rounded, her fear obvious.

"People react differently to the same kind of events,
sweetings. That poor woman needs our sympathy
more than anything. Charm's right. I'm proud of you
for what you did today. Now this Felicity will get help,
and not hurt anyone else," Granny Toogood said,
nodding thoughtfully.

"Charm, I should warn you—" Tulip began before
being interrupted by Doc Tanner's hand being
upraised.

"Enough, ladies, I need to get Charm to the lab for her
X-ray."

"Please don't rile up the crew with all of this," I
begged my family.

"They're pretty riled up already—a lynching not out
of the realm of possibility—but I'll see what I can do,"
Emma said, with her usual calm take-charge demeanor,
rather prized in the current situation.

"Thanks," I said then allowed Doc Tanner to escort
me from the crowded exam room into the corridor.

"Charm! Are you okay?" a chorus of voices erupted
and Doc gave them another raised hand.

"Ladies, ladies, that's what I'm trying to find out. I
suggest you all take a seat or go about your usual
business while *I* go about finding answers."

The chorus died down to a low rumble.

In the lab that contained the X-ray machine, we went
about getting the test done. I laid my arm carefully on
the area Doc indicated, then waited while the machine
did its thing.

"There, now, let's take a look."

I slid down off the stool and followed Doc Tanner to
the visual display on the monitor.

"Hmm, yes, there's a definite break in the radius. Fortunately, a clean break that should heal well. But we will have to immobilize it in a cast."

I could see the image clear as day on screen. Weird to see the inside of my own body projected there. Not nearly as detailed as the 3-D images I had full access to when dealing with others. Perhaps my view was more aligned with an MRI? I'd have to do some research.

I groaned at his words. "How long will the cast be on?" About the last thing I needed was to be out of commission for an extended period of time.

"A few weeks at least. Depends on how you heal." He talked as he worked, setting up the items he needed to secure my arm. "I heard you helped the two poison victims. Any truth to that?"

I bit my lip. "I was there and I did help a bit."

"What did you do?"

And so I explained, as best I could, while he set my arm and applied a clean white cast.

"You know, I believe you, Charm. I've seen miracles in my thirty years of doctoring. Things that medicine can't entirely account for. Most doctors don't talk about it, but it does happen. People's tumors shrinking unexpectedly, people coming around from flatlining that suggest that there is a continuation of the soul. A lot of talk about seeing a bright light where their relatives waited for them. Out of body experiences. A sense of something larger than themselves that embraces them with love and understanding. Who knows?" He shrugged, giving me a small smile. "But you are one remarkable young woman if you can help people in such a profound way. Just don't be taking away all my business now, eh." He gave a chuckle.

"No way I'm stepping on your toes, Doc. I'm just supplemental, at most." I shrugged, praying it stayed that way.

"You were interfering with a police investigation is how you got this broken arm, if I have my facts straight?"

My hackles rose. "If I hadn't, the murderer would still be on the loose."

"True, true. But you shouldn't put yourself at risk. Your family's counting on you."

He had a point, but the interfering comment kept me from saying it out loud.

"So, no cost to you then, this business with the helping the two poisoned men?" he pressed.

I shrugged. "A little. It's kind of exhausting."

He nodded sagely. "Of course. Just be careful, Charm. You've never been to see me before except for inoculations. It doesn't bode well."

I found myself nodding, even while knowing I would do all I could to help others. "I'll be careful, Doc."

"Okay, all done." He handed me a small sample and a prescription. "For pain. Don't exceed the recommended dosage. And come and see me if anything feels off. Okay?"

The waiting room had quieted down, I was grateful to discover when I exited the lab. My family and a few friends huddled in one area, their expressions heartwarmingly concerned. Granny Toogood caught sight of me first. "Sweeting, how are you doing? We're taking you home right now. You need to rest."

I nodded, finding myself choked up again. She gave me a hug, careful to avoid my broken left arm.

"Yeah, we're going to cover for you for the next few weeks while you heal. We're just making up a schedule now," Tulip spoke up, looking up from typing furiously on her compact laptop. Lots of nods accompanied her words. A few tears escaped this time. I rubbed them away furiously.

"It's going to be fine, Charm." Emma jumped up from one of the plastic orange chairs and stepped closer. Everyone crowded around for a group hug. I swallowed hard. *Best part of living in a small-town family – instant support.*

"Okay, okay. Enough already. Let's get Charm back to the café." Trust Star to get a grip first.

"Of course, Star can't be included past next week," Tulip said, giving a significant look.

I swung my head around to stare at Star. "Why's that?"

"Not now, Tulip, for goddess' sake." Star's face flushed pink under her tan.

"What is it, Star?" I asked pointedly. "What's going on?"

"She's been hired for a big role in a film in LA that starts in the spring. Isn't that marvelous?" Emma said, her eyes bright with excitement.

My worst fears were confirmed. I swore I needed to scrape my jaw up off the tiled hospital floor. "When were you going to tell me this?"

Star looked guilty as Hades. "Ah, well, soon."

I gritted my teeth together to prevent myself saying anything I couldn't come back from, then managed a few curt words. "Just take me home."

Back at the café, I kept my thoughts to myself, climbing up the endless stairs, one by one, to my apartment after telling everyone I needed to lie down. Propped up against the headboard of my bed, my sore arm positioned on a bed of pillows, I fell into a mental slump. This couldn't be happening. It wasn't fair. Breaking up our family like this? For what, a role in a darn movie?

What to do? Goddess, but this arm needed fixing. Angry, I laid my hand over the cast, but its thick whiteness obscured everything underneath. Darn it, I should have tried sooner, before the cast was applied. I had been afraid to try in case I healed the bone or bones in the wrong position. I mean, who knew how this worked? The thought just made me angrier, and I wanted to break the cumbersome thing off. If only I had a saw handy...

A light knock at the door drew my attention. Tulip poked her head around. "Can I come in?"

I shrugged. "Why not? Not like there's anything to be done, right?" I knew I was pouting, but I couldn't seem to help myself.

"I'm sorry I blurted it out like that. I should have known how you'd react. But, sis, it's Star's big break. We can't interfere. It wouldn't be right." She came closer and sat on the side of the bed.

I let out a deep breath, picking at the top of my coverlet. "Yeah, I know, but it still sucks." I had a sudden memory. "What were you meaning at the hospital? Something you wanted to tell me?"

She rolled her eyes and looked away, biting her lower lip. "Maybe now's not the time."

"No, I want to hear it, whatever it is. Please."

She let out a sigh. "You're not going to like it," she warned.

"What else is new? Just say it already"

"Well, you know the cat's out of the bag about your healing abilities?"

I nodded.

"And now everyone knows it's tied to your finding your true soul mate—the one you're supposed to be with, thanks to that girl Jennifer Morgan—or you lose the gift, right?"

I nodded, gritting my teeth. "According to Granny and the legend, yeah."

"Well, there's a plot against you and Constable Collins to keep you two apart. No one wants you to lose your healing gift."

"What? That's crazy!" My anger spilled over in a new direction. How dare they!

"I just thought you should know, in case weird stuff begins to happen."

My mind seized on the information. No way were they going to get away with any shenanigans concerning me and Ace, I'd see to that. Talk about self-serving, egotistical, hypocritical...

I gave Tulip a sweet smile, slitting my eyes, as I came up with the perfect plan. "Thanks for sharing, sis. You can leave it with me."

Her eyes widened with concern. "Ah—why aren't you mad? What are you going to do about it?"

"No worries. And please tell the bride and groom I'll be bringing a plus one to the wedding on Saturday. Constable Ace Collins in the flesh." And what perfect man flesh, all handsome and hot as Hades. And I'd show the town what a steamy romance looked like.

"Charm, do you think that's wise?"

"I need to rest now." I shooed her away with a wave of my hand. And even though I couldn't see anything inside the loathsome cast, I sent all my happy, healing vibes into it before falling dead asleep.

Morning came too early. A knock at the door and Granny opened it, carrying a tray. "Are you awake, sweeting?"

"Mmm, yes, ma'am."

She smiled and came closer. "I brought you some breakfast. You need help eating or washing? Something for the pain?"

"No, it's doing a lot better, thanks. I'll be fine, don't worry." I sat up straighter.

"Good." She set the tray down on my lap. "I've put a bell on the tray. Just dingle if you need something, okay? I'll leave you to eat in peace."

"Sure, thanks."

She gave me a kiss on the cheek and exited, closing the door softly behind her.

I ate with gusto down to the last bite of the fluffy scrambled eggs, warm fresh croissants and steaming hot coffee. Satiated, I lay back and sent more healing thoughts into my left arm. It tingled a bit, then felt warmer and much better. Hmm, maybe there was hope yet for this cast coming off sooner than expected? The pain was almost gone and I didn't need any medicine. I just wished I could see inside the darn cast. Of course, an itch broke out and I wanted to tear it off to get at it. But itching meant it was healing, right?

Two days until the wedding. Would they be enough?

Chapter Twenty-Four

The morning of the wedding proved drizzly and overcast, dampening discussion around the breakfast table. For two days now my family had been convening together in the morning. I liked it, more than I could say. Of course, the elephant in the room was Star's leaving. But no one had broached the subject again and I vastly preferred to pretend it wasn't happening. I mean, the movie business was fickle — they could cancel her chance at any moment. I had a guilty start, realizing how many spells I had sort of been casting to the skies in the hopes that that was exactly what would happen. *Some things are best kept to one's self.*

"I'm going to the hospital today to have Doc Tanner look at my arm. I want him to check something."

"I'll drive you," Star said too quickly, getting a gleam in her eye. She wanted me alone. To talk. And I didn't want to.

"I thought it was your turn to open the café this morning?" I said, praying it was true.

"No, not my turn." She gave me a curt reply and grabbed her purse. "If you're ready, let's go. We've got hair appointments this morning. An afternoon wedding makes things so tight," she grumbled.

I got up and put my dishes into the sink, preparing to wash them.

"Get going, I'll take care of things here," Tulip said, pushing me away from the counter and taking over.

"Thanks," I replied, wishing I could find another way to delay the inevitable. I sighed. No choice but to follow Star out of the kitchen and into the alley where Thor awaited. It felt odd, getting into the passenger side.

Star got in and waited while I buckled up. "Charm, we need to talk."

"I know. But could it wait until after the wedding, please?"

She gave me a sigh of frustration and started Thor's motor. "Okay, but you can't ignore it, because it's going to happen whether you want it to or not. I want to go away with your blessing. It's my one chance at the big time, and I would like my sisters to be okay with it. To wish me well. If I don't do it now, I might be stuck in Snowy Lake forever."

"Is that so bad? Being stuck here? It's a great place to be."

"I know, for you. But I'm not you or Tulip. I've dreamed of becoming famous since I was a little girl. To share my talents with the world. You do that, share your talents and gifts with others. Why not me?"

"What! People *love* to hear you sing. You've made so many of them happy right here in Snowy Lake. You don't need to go away."

"You're impossible to talk to. You know that?"

I clamped my mouth shut.

At the hospital, I jumped out. "I'll see myself back."

"Fine." She drove off in a cloud of righteous anger.

I stomped through the sliding glass doors of the hospital entrance, feeling quite put upon. Surely someone could talk some sense into my sister? Maybe Granny could help. Hollywood was not the place for an innocent like Star. They'd eat her up and spit her out. I shuddered. That den of wolves had no draw for me. It was scarier than the timber wolves around our town.

"Is Dr. Tanner available, Stacey?" I asked at the front desk.

"I'll check."

"Thanks."

She picked up the house phone and spoke a few words before setting it back down. "Yes, and he can see you right now. How are you doing, by the way?"

"Good, thanks." I hurried down the hallway to the doctor's office.

"Charm. Nice to see you doing so well. What brings you by so soon? Are you in more pain?"

"I want you to check my arm. I think it's healed."

"What? That's impossible."

"Please, I just need you to X-ray it again. I'm pretty certain."

He shook his head. "Okay, if it makes you feel better, I'll do it. But don't expect any miracles, okay?"

I grinned at him. "Always, Doc, always."

Ten minutes later and my balloon popped. "The break's just beginning to mend. But it's going to be a few more weeks, I'm afraid. That was a serious break, Charm."

"Phhht. Well, that sucks." *I can only help heal others but not myself? Who writes these rules?*

Five minutes and I was back out on the street, headed at a steady jog toward the Clip Joint. Might as well be first in line. *Let's face it, Susie has her work cut out for her this morning.* I hadn't even shampooed in two days.

"Good morning, Charm." Susie Diamond's bright smile greeted me. The air was heavily scented with a bouquet of strange fragrances that tickled my olfactory sense. I sneezed once, twice, three times in succession, my usual number.

"Mornin', Susie. You're looking beautiful," I said, wiping my teary eyes. And she did. Golden and pink curls arranged perfectly around her cherub features brought out her sublime complexion. "I could use a whole lot of your expertise today. I haven't had time to do much grooming lately."

"Tsk-tsk. My goodness, look at you, hon. Well, what's to be expected with a cast on. But you've come to the right place." She glanced at my wounded wing. "We need to decorate that sucker. It's so plain."

I grinned, holding up my left hand. "That's a good idea. Got any flower decals?"

"I do. I'm thinking red roses intertwined with garland." Her rosebud lips pursed, she tilted her head to the side.

I gave a grin. "Perfect. Let's get this sucker covered up before I end up with a thousand drunken scrawled signatures at the wedding."

"I'll say. Come, sit down at the shampoo sink and we'll get you started right now before the rush begins."

"Thanks, that's what I was hoping for. That, and a miracle to make me presentable for the wedding party." I grimaced and sat down on the chair in front of the sink.

"Well, not going to be easy, but I'll haul out my big bag of tricks." The twinkle in her eyes softened the blow.

And did she haul out her bag of tricks. An hour or so later, I hardly recognized myself in the mirror. Perfect dark curls flowed all around my shoulders, held back with a few deep red rosebuds strategically placed around my hairline. The flowers matched the color of the bridesmaid dresses and the ones newly decorating my cast, one of the few colors that flattered me and made me feel pretty.

"Wow, you are a miracle worker. Thanks, Susie." I jumped up and kissed her on the cheek, careful not to smudge her makeup.

I paid, leaving a generous tip for the extra pampering. The door burst open and we both turned to check who had entered. Jennifer Morgan stood there, looking all too pleased with herself.

"Morning. I thought I'd get in early for my appointment—beat the rush," she said, a wide grin accompanying her words.

I nodded, not trusting myself to speak.

"Have you heard the amazing news?" she asked.

By the self-satisfied glow, I had to assume the worst. *But please, don't let it be a bonanza.* That would suck.

"No," Susie said, closing the till with enough force that it groaned on impact. "What's up?"

Jennifer looked at me, dying to share, but waiting to give it even more import by wasting a few precious seconds.

That bugged me. *Big time.* "Did you happen to find a basket of scruples out there with your name on it?" I asked.

That annoyed her. *Good.* She narrowed her eyes, her lips twitching. "I do apologize for any inconvenience I may have inadvertently put you through. I had no idea I wasn't suppose to share such an important bit of knowledge. But I would think you'd want everyone to know about your gift anyway, since you'll be sharing it." She dismissed my objections with far too much ease.

I gritted my teeth over her glossing over confidentiality concerns. And I certainly didn't want to discuss Ace with her. *So, a betrayer and a liar to boot. Nice friend.* "Yes, but not all of it. That was wrong, sharing my private personal stuff with my neighbors."

She was unrepentant. "Well, neither here nor there now. Because I have made the find of the century!"

"What's that?" Susie asked while I silently fumed.

"The mother lode."

Figures. But then, it could be good for our town. Maybe the trickle-down effect of extra capital would help with a few street repairs? Thor's suspension was always taking a beating, dancing in and out of potholes.

"Well, that's some news," Susie said. "Too bad I already heard it earlier."

Jennifer's face screwed up with annoyance. "How could you know?" she sputtered.

"Charm's Auntie T.J. came by for a hairdo at seven. Old news by now, I'm afraid, my dear." Susie dismissed her with a condescending glance.

"Well, I think I'll just take my business elsewhere," she said.

"No worries," Susie said. "I have a busy day without having to do your scuzzy hair, darlin'."

Jennifer left in a huff.

"You know she'll just go complain to Ace about us, right?" I said.

"So? She'll soon be gone anyway."

"How do you figure that?"

Susie reached down and picked up something from behind her reception desk. She held up a familiar effigy. "Poppets. They're all over town now and together they make us strong. A big wind will soon blow that wicked witch back east and right out of your hair, hon."

I began to laugh, then found it hard to stop.

"Careful, you'll ruin your beautiful makeup," Susie warned, though she was laughing right alongside me.

I left the salon still giggling. The women had circled the wagons and Miss Jennifer Morgan didn't stand a chance. *Well, maybe. Best laid plans and all that.* If I'd learned anything so far, it was that the universe could turn on a dime. The thought sobered me up and I pushed through the front door at the Tea & Tarot in a more reflective mood. Now that the murder was solved, what was next? Hmm. Operation keep Star at home? The angels tsk-tsked over the doorway, not bothering to sing. *Yeah, guilty.*

The café hummed with activity. Star looked up from serving a customer. "Wow. You cleaned up nice, sis."

"Thanks. Suzy worked her magic. Have you seen Granny?"

"She was here a few minutes ago. Might be in the back."

"Thanks," I said, striding right on by a few customers who turned to stare and into the kitchen.

"Sweeting, my goodness, your cast looks pretty. And don't you look beautiful," Granny said, looking up from sipping a cup of herbal tea at the kitchen table.

Auntie T.J. was buzzing around, rinsing a few dishes. She nodded her approval of my appearance.

"Time you fixed yourself up, if you ever want to find a man."

"Yup, Susie's a miracle worker." I ignored my auntie's dig.

Granny's eyebrows raised over her all-knowing blue eyes. "Well, not hard to achieve. You were a beautiful child and now you're even more lovely as a young woman. Other than your stubborn streak, you were an easy child to raise."

"Can I talk to you?" I said, plunking myself down.

"Sure, what's up?"

"It's about Ace and —"

The phone rang loudly, interrupting.

"I'll get it," Auntie T.J. said.

"You and Constable Collins at odds again?" Granny asked.

"Not exactly. But something weird happened." I hesitated, not certain I wanted confirmation.

"Yes?" she prompted.

"Well, do you think it's even possible to read another's mind? You know, hear their thoughts without their speaking?"

"Is that what's happening between you and Ace? Telepathy?"

I nodded. "So weird, I'm getting a few of his thoughts drifting in. Can't do it on demand or anything like that." I shuddered. "I just don't want it to get any worse."

"That's rather significant, all right." She smiled, disarming me, and nodding her approval.

"Yeah, thought you'd say that. But how significant is it?"

"How significant do you think it is?"

I hesitated, finding it hard to admit to aloud.

"I think—"

"Oh lord, no!" Auntie T.J.'s stricken tone stopped our conversation in its tracks.

I swiveled my head around to check her out. Her usually robust complexion was as pale as I'd ever seen anyone.

"What is it? What's wrong, sister?" Granny asked.

She left the phone off the hook and wobbled her way to our table, sinking down onto a chair, placing her hand over her chest as though it was hard for her to take a breath.

"What is it?" I asked, imagining the worst. "What do you want me to do? Is it your heart?"

She shook her head slowly back and forth. "No, I'm fine. Physically at least. I don't know if I should say."

"Spill it, Tegan Jane. Who's on the phone?"

She stood up straighter and bit her lip. "It's your mother, Charm. She wants to speak to you."

My worst fears realized. A ghost from the past rising up and choking me. I stood abruptly, knocking my chair over in the process. It clattered to the floor. I didn't care. I had to get away. *Why now? Why come back now?*

I ran. Out through the back door and into the alley. I dimly heard voices calling after me, but I couldn't stop. I had to get away. I needed time alone.

I got into Thor and slumped back against the seat. A few minutes to gather myself was all I asked for. Why was my mother doing this? After all these years? She had no right. Everyone would be upset by her return. Maybe she wasn't returning? I sat up straighter. Auntie T.J. said she just wanted to talk to me.

Yeah, maybe she wanted to apologize on the phone? Because if she came back, she'd drive Star, and maybe even Tulip, away. Would I leave too? No. Snowy Lake was my home. Nothing and no one person would ever take that away from me. No way.

A noise at the side of the Jeep woke me from my reverie. I glanced over and there was Ace opening the passenger door and climbing inside. He turned and stared at me, his expression softened by concern. I swallowed, finding it difficult to look him in the eyes.

"How you doing, darlin'?" He reached over and threaded his hand into a stray curl on my shoulder, lifting it and letting it slip through his fingers. I shivered.

"Cold?" He reached over and drew me to him, hugging me against his broad chest. I took a deep breath, his scent flooding me with a sense of peace. And need. My body began to vibrate with the unexpected sensation. I suddenly wanted more. Much more than just Ace having his arms around me.

I knew I should push him away, but I longed for just a few more precious minutes without the outside world interfering. My skin was electrified with the good feeling I couldn't possibly describe. Words fell short. No way any romantic writer could match it. It was that amazing. "I'm better. Thanks."

"You want to talk about it?"

"Nothing to talk about."

"Never too soon to share a worry, darlin'."

I took a deep breath. I might as well spill. He'd know all of it soon anyway.

"My mother, who abandoned us with Granny Toogood when we were eight — but you know that part already — just called the café. Wants to talk to me. I don't know why. I just got out of there. I panicked, I guess." *And Star wants to leave us.*

I felt the breath leave his body in a deep sigh. "I'm sorry. Not sure what to say about that. Kind of out of left field for you. And not really something one can prepare for easily."

"No kidding. I'm not even sure how to feel."

"There's no right way or wrong way. Just stay true to you. All anyone can manage."

"I don't know what's going to happen—what will befall us if she comes back into our lives." I heard the slight whiney sound, but I couldn't help it.

"We'll cross that bridge when we come to it. You know I care about you, very, very much, Miss McCall. I promise I'll be here for you. Always." He hesitated before adding. "You know Star has to follow her own path."

His words took my breath clear away. When I found my voice again, it trembled with emotion. "Thank you. I think that's one of the nicest things anyone's ever said to me." I sniffed, tears welling up. "But I can't hold you to that." I ignored his thoughts on my sister, but I caught a glimpse of them.

"Aw, darlin', don't cry. Of course you can. No matter where I am in this world, you call me, and I promise to be there. Anytime. Anyplace. You have my word as an officer and a gentleman."

"An officer and a gentleman, eh?" A strength welled up inside me, even while I giggled at his use of a cliché movie title. Yes. I could do anything knowing Ace was in my corner. I gave a quick thank you to the whole darn universe. If ever I needed a boost, this was that time. Maybe I could move forward. And let Star go do what she must.

He gave me a gentle smile and my body filled with emotion. *Yes.* He was the man for me. I knew it in my bones right then, and in my heart. The head rush that followed the realization left me stunned for a second.

Then I reached up and touched his chiseled jawline, ran my fingers over his face, memorizing each dip and valley. Touched his thick soft, tousled hair. For once he wasn't wearing his hat. His warmth penetrated my fingers, sent a delicious burst of electricity arcing through my veins. It was then that I saw it. A tiny feather tucked around a lock of hair. It must have fallen onto him at some point this morning. I reached up and plucked it off, laying it on the dash to add to my memory box.

"Thank you for being you," I said before tipping my head up and closing my eyes. "Now kiss me, Sheriff."

He needed no second invitation. He leaned in, capturing my willing lips with his ever-so-perfect mouth. Our tongues tangoed in the ancient mating ritual, my body melting with acute need. A loud popping sound echoed in my ears.

"What was that?" Ace said, pulling his lips away. I tugged on the back of his neck, drawing him to me, not wanting the kiss to end.

"Probably just a light bulb exploding. Nothing to worry about," I murmured. "Happens all the time around me."

He gave a slight shrug, resuming our kiss. *Yes.* My soul swelled up inside me, seeming to meld with his in some kind of swirling, divine cloud dance. It felt as if all our atoms were aligning, setting things in their proper order.

Life. It just doesn't get any better than this…

Epilogue

Auntie T.J. came flying into the café, jarring the angels overhead and making them squeal in wild delight. Our auntie's round face was aglow with news. *Must be important.* She usually just called.

"Guess who bought an early home pregnancy kit?"

The three of us had just sat down for a coffee to check out the new wedding photos. The past two weeks had been insane since Melody and Mick's wedding. Only one fight at the reception, so it hadn't even come close to the most memorable event in recent history. A knock-down, drag-out fight between the groom's mother and Melody's Auntie Beth over the choice of topper for the groom's cake hardly registered on anyone's radar. *Probably best not to choose chubby figurines that insult the bride's robust figure.* And we did have the luxury of each stage of the event captured in living color, right down to the cake-in-the-face part when Auntie Beth got the upper hand over her rival. But between catering at the movie set, where I'd been putting up with Mimi's barely concealed hostility, and keeping up with business in the café while worrying about the future for Star and my family, I'd hardly had time for my favorite Mountie. Just thinking about him, though, brought a smile to my lips. *And have I said what a great kisser he is…?*

"Who, Auntie?" Tulip bit for the three of us.

"You have to guess! No fun in just sayin' it." She placed her hands on her ample hips and gave a snort.

"What do we get if we guess it right?"

Auntie T.J. narrowed her eyes at me. "You know about this?"

"Maybe," I said with a coy smile. "Let's see — I'd bet Christine Blackmore. Right?"

"Harrumph. You must have cheated." She pursed her lips.

I shook my head. "Nope." Healing her certainly hadn't been cheating in my opinion. The gift was goddess given and approved.

"Well, I think that's great. Doesn't matter how it happened. I'm so happy for her and Sean. They've been wanting a baby for ages," Tulip said.

"Me too," Star said.

"Me three," I added with a wide grin. I looked around the café, enjoying watching Tom and Charlie argue about whose turn it was to pay. *Ah, normalcy.* Everything was all right with the world. At least for this moment. And tomorrow could take care of itself — with the help of a little magic, of course.

Want to see more from this author?
Here's a taster for you to enjoy!

The TETRAD Group:
Racing Peril
January Bain

Excerpt

Jake Marshall squinted behind his dark sunglasses. *What was that?* Even with the world's worst hangover, he'd caught the glint of light reflecting from a distant object. Discreetly pulling out his Steiner Ranger Xtreme binoculars from his jacket pocket, he brought them up to his face, focusing their ultra-high resolution on the roof of what looked like a strip mall a full city block away from the courthouse. He moved the optical device back and forth, checking all along the flat roofline and the squat structure of an air conditioner and vent, watching intently for another glimmer. It didn't come, but he couldn't shake the feeling of unease that had settled in his gut. And his gut never lied.

I should have listened to it the day I met Racheal. Note to self, never override instinct again. He'd been flattered such a gorgeous woman had come on to him, acting as if she couldn't live without a tumble in the hay. *A man can't be blamed for the direction his cock takes him in, right?* But it had turned out to be a very bad decision. Worse, he'd known better. And no amount of drinking was going to stop the pain caused by her having ditched him while he was away doing his duty for his country. Coming home to surprise her and catching her in bed with some guy named Sean *Shithead* Kincaid — that had hurt like hell. And still did. And now here he was on leave from his military regiment in Canada, filling in for a friend on the steps of a LA courthouse.

And this job. He shook his head at the stupidity of some people. Why would the guy expose himself to a press conference when slinking away into the night would better suit the situation? The asshole had gotten off on a technicality, after all. Nothing to be proud of unless it was the fact that his rich father could afford the best lawyer in town. Gloating was not smart. Jake's gut agreed.

The job of guarding the asshole they were presently waiting to escort to his daddy's hideaway had fallen to him when his school chum had come down with the worst case of flu Jake had ever witnessed. He'd stepped up. Had to and wanted to. As if he could have done otherwise, when Max had taken him in when he'd turned up on his doorstep a week ago, needing a change of scenery. And not today he was filling in for Max's own private firm, Sterling Security, as payback for all the guy had done for him, and he didn't intend to fuck it up. Jake's hangover made no odds, not when Max Sterling deserved Jake's A-game.

Max's change in direction had gone smoothly — hell, maybe *he* should start thinking seriously about leaving the army now. Three tours had taken it out of him. And that sent him, just like that, back to Afghanistan, back to the worst horror of his life, back to the reason for his PTSD.

* * * *

They'd landed outside the wire enclosing the compound of Joint Task Force 2, the special operations branch of the Canadian military he'd been assigned to in Afghanistan, ready to dig in and do his part, tasked with toppling the Taliban regime. *Operation Scorpion*. Capable of doing exactly what it implied — to both sides. Just the how and the when were beyond his control.

A remote shriek sounded as he walked toward the compound. It grew in intensity, an unstoppable freight train, hurling closer by the second. An aircraft flew directly overhead, its wake disturbing the air, then a second later, a dull thud came. The ground trembled. A small pall of smoke rose in the distance. The shriek faded.

Then another shriek ripped the air. One he could pinpoint this time, coming from a northern ridge. The shriek grew to a wail, a harpy screaming in retribution. The ground shook uncontrollably and men began running.

Lieutenant Gibson, a junior officer and squad leader, shouted, "Incoming! Get inside the wire! Run! Now!"

His words threw ice water into Jake's face. A single word connected with his brain. *Run.*

Racing to the side entrance to get inside the camp, he struggled for each breath. He was not used to the lack of oxygen at the high altitude. *Oh, God.* What needed doing first?

Captain Krill raced into view, gesturing for him to follow. "Some kids got hit from these rounds. They're at the front gates."

His began moving, running after Krill, wanting to go faster still, lungs burning. He followed the captain around the corner and thirty yards away some of his fellow soldiers were opening the front gate. Crying, distraught Afghan civilians began pouring through. He kept running.

Then he saw the kids. Heard their screams. Some thrashing in agony in their parents' arms, others lying still. He dropped his rifle, tore off his helmet and dumped his body armor in the dirt. Sprinted the last stretch.

"Grab them!" one of the soldiers screamed over the din.

A loud argument broke out, slowing them down.

"They're insisting you take the boys first," one of the soldiers explained, a translator who understood what Jake couldn't.

"Take them all!" Krill ordered.

Other soldiers picked up the few left alive while Jake scooped up the nearest child, turning to follow the others to the aid station. He glanced down at the child after a few steps. A little girl, no more than five, so light in his arms he almost thought he'd imagined her. She wore a dress made of burlap, rough to the touch, and had bright emerald-green eyes, deep and filled with pain, and long raven hair plastered to her skin from tears and blood.

He kept running, cradling her head and shoulders in his right hand, her slight body pressed against his ribs, a thigh by his left forearm. Her tiny arm flailed about. She gasped, screaming again and again, never stopping.

"Shush, it's okay. It's okay, little one," he said it over and over as he ran, each step an agony of taking too fucking long.

An image of his niece seared his brain. Cute as a button with big blue eyes and long brown curls. Dressed up in a fancy dress for Sunday School and giving him the biggest grin. Emily was about this girl's age. Maybe a little older.

Keep moving.

Her breathing changed. Grew ragged. Her screams lessened. Her eyes were growing dull. She stared up at him, this stranger in the uniform, and her abject terror faded.

Warmth spread down his chest. What was it? His legs operated on autopilot as he ran, his eyes fixed on hers.

She screamed one last time, the sound hoarse and weak. The warmth spread to his hip and trickled down his thighs. What was it?

He had to look. When he did, his brain shut down. Horror consumed him at the one tiny bare foot, perfectly formed and covered in brown dust, and the other a torn chunk of burnt flesh below her dimpled kneecap. A bloody stump. A white bone jutted through the ruined skin and muscle. Horror. Beyond all horrors.

He stumbled, lost his stride. The little girl let out a shaking breath, dark and raspy.

"It's-okay-it's-okay-it's-okay."

One more step. One more step.

Her neck grew slack under his arm. The warmth spread down his body.

He glanced down once more. Her fear gone, the spark of life gone. All gone.

The world around him dropped away. Muffled. Soldiers ran by in slow motion. Parents cried in the distant. Others barked orders he could no longer hear, the horror in his head masking everything else.

Home of Erotic Romance

Sign up for our newsletter and find out about all our romance book releases, eBook sales and promotions, sneak peeks and FREE romance books!

About the Author

January Bain has wished on every falling star, every blown-out birthday candle and every coin thrown in a fountain to be a storyteller. To share the tales of high adventure, mysteries, and full-blown thrillers she has dreamed of all her life. The story you now have in your hands is the compilation of a lot of things manifesting itself for this special series. Hundreds of hours spent researching the unusual and the mundane have come together to create a series that features strong women who don't take life too seriously, wild adventures full of twists and unforeseen turns, and hot complicated men who aren't afraid to take risks. She can only hope the stories of her beloved Brass Ringers will capture your imagination as much as they did hers when she wrote them.

If you are looking for January Bain, you can find her hard at work every morning without fail in her office with two furry babies trying to prove who does a better job of guarding the doorway. And, of course, she's married to the most romantic man! Who once famously replied to her inquiry about buying fresh flowers for their home every week, "Give me one good reason why not?" Leaving her speechless and knocking her head against the proverbial wall for being so darn foolish. She loves flowers.

January loves to hear from readers. You can find her contact information, website details and author profile page at https://www.totallybound.com